THE SIREN SERIES

SiRen's End

USA TODAY BESTSELLING AUTHOR
JESSICA CAGE

3

Written by Jessica Cage

Edited by Debbi Watson
Additional Editing by Joseph Editorial Services
Cover Design by: Solidarity Graphics
Book Design by: Jessica Cage

ISBN-13: **978-1-958295-25-0**

DEDICATION

To my best friend who refuses to allow
me to give up on myself.

I love you and I am so proud of you.

ᴀCKNOWLEDGMENTS

I have to acknowledge Debbi Watson. A wonderful editor who helps to make my projects even better! Also to the many authors and other members of the writing community who continue to support and inspire me.

Thank you!

Prologue

Life is such a fragile thing. That's a lesson that was always shoved down my throat. Coals of furious fire burned my esophagus as it traveled to land in my gut and sear a mark on my soul forever. I would never be the same.

Never had I imagined that things could go so badly. Everyone was trying to help me. That's all they ever did. Try to help me. Once again, I stood watching my friends, the ones I loved; die at the hands of the man who gave me life as I held on to the hand of my mother for dear life. I'd lost her once, lived my life without her. I didn't want to lose her again, but I couldn't allow my friends to sacrifice their lives for me.

"FATHER!" I screamed into the night before everything shattered.

CHAPTER
I

"*Are you sure we're doing the right thing?* It's not like she is going to welcome me with open arms. I'm not just another friend you're bringing home." My stomach was already in knots, and it only got worse with each piece of clothing I stuffed into my bag.

"Sy, I told you, my mother is not like the other witches of the coven. Think about it. She sent me away from our people because she didn't want me to adapt to their backwards standards." Rhys smiled and pulled me close to him. The soft kiss on my cheek sent a flow of warmth across my body and momentarily pushed away my worries. "My mother will welcome you into her world, just as I have."

"Sure, it's easy for you to assume that now, but how can you be so sure?" We'd been over this decision a hundred times, and yet I was still just as nervous as the first time he suggested with go to his mother's house for safety.

"She told me once, in secret, that she never agreed with what they did to your family. My mother isn't the kind to punish someone for what others did long before they were even born. You had no hand in what your ancestors did, or even what your father is planning on doing now." He lifted my chin with his finger to look me in the eye. "None of this is your fault. Trust me, my mother doesn't hold any of this against you."

"Yeah, I get that part. She won't hold other people's actions against me, but what about my own?" I pulled away from his hug and moved back to the bed where my half-packed bag waited. "She'll judge me for the evil things I've done, Rhys."

"What evil have you done?" He scoffed and returned to his task of packing his own bag.

Of course, to Rhys I could do no wrong, but there was so much that weighed on my conscience. Everyone had their own demons. This was not a rule that I was exempt from. I'd taken lives. I'd broken hearts and turned family members against one another. How could that not count as evil?

"Existing for one." That answer should have at least been obvious to him. Okay, it wasn't technically my doing, but by simply being alive, according to just about every person I had come in contact with in recent months, I was actively taking part in the damnation of the entire world.

"Stop, please." He paused as he looked at me. There was more that he wanted to say, but our intrusive house guest pushed the door open.

"Yes, please stop. I love you guys, but your somber vibe is really getting tough to ignore!" Maggie spoke up from outside of our room door. She held a large duffle bag swung over her shoulder. "We ready to roll or not?"

"Ah, great, you've awakened the beast." Rhys rolled his eyes. He still wasn't a fan of Maggie.

He had good reason for it. The woman nearly broke his leg right before she kidnapped me for three days.

"Hilarious, lover boy." She tossed him the keys.

After holding me hostage to be judged by the ancestors, the coven conveniently assigned Maggie to be my guardian. She was there to make sure that I didn't step out of line. If I made one wrong move, she was to report it back to them so they could swiftly punish me for it.

"Look, everything will be fine. Trust me."

I wanted to trust his intuition. I really did. Every part of me hoped he was right, that driving into the heart of New Orleans, a place known for its supernatural beings even in human communities, was a good idea. The hard part was I learned to trust that little nudge in my belly, that thing telling me I was heading for complete and total disaster.

Hell, who knows? Maybe this time it would be wrong.

~*~

One thing was good; the witches were true to their word. Not once did anyone try to stop us as we headed for the home of Mardi Gras. Part of me expected the High Council to intervene, but the spiritual ancestors of the coven told them to keep a distance. Marlo, the old witch who ran the coven, made it perfectly clear how she felt about me.

Maggie, our newest companion on this journey, sat in the back seat with headphones that covered her ears and blasted whatever rock music was playing on Pandora at the moment. As the scenery sped past the window in a blend of trees and vegetation, my hearing picked up everything from the tapping of Rhys' fingertips on the steering wheel to the slight lag in the back tire that needed air. I could see far enough into the distance to tell that we were being watched by werewolves. As we passed through their territory, they disappeared. They wanted no trouble and they wouldn't approach us, but they also wouldn't allow us to set up camp there, not that we ever intended to.

The extensive list of hidden species and paranormal occurrences that I'd learned about since finding out about my true self was astounding and unsettling. To top it all off, the only advice given to me regarding coping with these revelations was to accept that all things, even the ones I once felt were impossible, were, in fact, plausible and more than likely real. It was that, or battle with the uncertainty until I lost my sanity.

That shouldn't have been that difficult, considering how pretty hypocritical it was to think about anything else. How could I talk about what shouldn't exist when I was the hybrid seed born of a siren and a warlock? What I also had to accept was that my old life was long gone and too far out of reach. Friends and family who I adored were off limits to me now.

To contact them would mean introducing the danger of a supernatural ticking time bomb into their lives. I'd already worked so hard to prevent that from happening. Luckily, it would seem my friends were doing just fine without me. I'd been able to check in on them once and though they missed me, they were okay. Their lives were still normal.

As for my family, well, the one member I would have attempted to contact, my aunt, was no longer a friend of mine. Noreen turned out to be my enemy. She was the one who started the downward spiral that my life had become. Unfortunately, she was also the only family I had left.

It would be a bald-faced lie to say that if I ever saw her again, she wouldn't be the first to receive a taste of the power that everyone feared. Of course, that would mean breaking my promise to the coven spirits and being hunted down like a wild animal again. Somehow, she just didn't seem worth it. However, to fantasize about her suffering for her betrayal was satisfying. I would often think about it whenever my current situation weighed on me. Nothing lifted my spirits quite like a well-executed revenge plot, even if it was only in my imagination.

"I have to pee." Maggie spoke from the back seat and began tapping on the back of Rhys' headrest. He sighed, flashed an angry stare at her in the rearview mirror, and pulled off the highway at the nearest exit.

"Make it quick." Rhys shot Maggie another glare, and she returned fire by sticking her tongue out and blowing raspberries his way. By the way they bickered, I could tell those two would be the best of friends. "I guess I might as well as fuel up while we're here. Do you need anything from inside?" He tapped me on the knee.

"No, I'm good. Thanks." I smiled and watched them head into the station.

With Rhys and Maggie away, my head tuned in to a symphony of terrible thoughts that became the backdrop to my rising fears. No matter how I tried to push the doubts away, they returned, pummeling me from within. Chaotic ideas and worries came hurling at me from every direction. What was I really walking into? Why did my gut tell me that going to New Orleans would lead to disaster? Why did it also tell me I had to go? How many people would suffer because of my decision?

Was it selfish to expect Rhys and his mother to help me? After everything I'd done to prove I wasn't a monster, it felt like I was going against that. Marlo and the witches would be all too eager to come barging in, ready to cut me down. The car was suddenly too cramped and became stuffy. I climbed out of the car to stretch my limbs. The second my feet touched the ground, I felt centered again. With my back against the door, I closed my eyes and soaked up the warm rays of the sun.

'Syrinada'

The eerie voice, the mimic of a breeze tickling my

ear drum, spoke my name. Ignoring it was like trying to avoid scratching a mosquito bite. No matter how much cocoa butter you covered it with, soothing away the irritation, it was still there, and eventually your nails would scrape the surface to bring sweet yet temporary satisfaction.

'Syrinada.'

The voice was familiar, or more accurately put, it was the ghost of a voice that was familiar. I'd heard it before, yet I couldn't place the sound. With my eyes closed tight and my focus zoned in on it, I tried to dig into the recesses of my mind. It belonged to a woman, but who was she? Her physical existence would remain a mystery, no matter how hard I searched. Besides, my senses could pick up every being within a ten-mile radius, and she was not one of them.

The trippy part about my powers, the part that really got to me, was not the part about being able to lure people to me, but being able to sense them, all the souls that surrounded me. They were like beacons. I could feel them, their strength, their desires. It was overwhelming, but I learned more and more each day to control it.

The woman who the voice belong to wasn't one of the beacons I felt in my surroundings. Her essence was in the air, but her physical presence was not. Even then, her essence faded. Twice, that was it, no haunting

8

continuation of the call. She said my name twice and by the time Rhys returned from the store, all evidence of the eerie presence ceased to exist.

"We're all set." Rhys finished pumping the gas. Maggie was back in her rightful place, stretched out across the back seat, and our drive continued on.

Still, I felt as though his mother wouldn't accept me. His hopes were high, and I'd resolved myself to not take that from him. There were bigger things for me to be worried about. There was no way to deny that by returning to New Orleans I would set off a series of events that would very well work as a domino effect, with the last piece to fall being the destruction of whatever I had kept secure in my life. Regardless, it had to be done. I couldn't live my life on the run forever.

JESSICA CAGE

CHAPTER
2

The old house sat in the middle of the ruins of old New Orleans, untouched by the disaster that tore apart a once thriving community. Quite like the other houses owned by witches and other supernatural beings. Driving through the area, we passed by houses that seemed out of place, surrounded by wastelands. Each looked as good as the day they were first constructed. The witches were sure to protect themselves when the storm hit.

"This is it, home." Rhys grabbed the bag from the back of the trunk and threw it over his shoulder. Maggie did the same, and I grabbed one of my own.

His house reminded me of the one I stayed in during my first visit to the city with the Denali brothers, my mermen protectors. It stood proud, two stories with a large porch that wrapped around to the back deck. It was grand, and it reminded me of the pictures of plantation homes. The image used to fill me with sorrow, but now knowing that not all were the houses of horror, and how much magic dwelled within the walls of such places, I was excited to step foot inside.

"It's a shame. All this land still sits like this, total chaos." Maggie scanned the area as she stretched her limbs. "I never get over it."

"Why didn't the witches protect more? Why not forge against the storm together?" I gave voice to the question that felt obvious.

"That would have brought too much attention, Syrinada. Imagine the entire world watching an entire city become submerged beneath the waters, only to reemerge completely unharmed."

He was right, not only would that alert every human, but other forces as well; evil ones who would come and try to gain the power that the covens possessed. That was a risk that was far too great.

"Even our homes, to the human eye, looked like they were in total disrepair for a short time." Rhys continued. "Gradually we lifted the veils so that it would appear we had repaired the damage that was done over time, not overnight." Rhys stopped and stared as we did; a moment of remembrance for all that they lost.

"I understand. You did what you could, what made sense." I watched him closely.

"Trust me." He looked at me. "We wanted to help, to do more, but we couldn't. If we had, it would have meant putting the covens at risk. And mort than that, anyone who helped would have faced severe punishment."

"From the ancestors?" I asked, thinking of the spirits I met before.

"Yes," he confirmed. "All the people that believe witches are yet another thing of fairy tales would have turned on us and hunted us down. It wouldn't have mattered how many lives we'd saved. History has taught us that much. There would have been a war with humans, as they would no longer consider us a part of them.

"Think about it. How long do you think it would have taken them to realize that we aren't the only ones who are different? How long before they discovered all the other supernatural species that are out there? This was bigger than us."

"I can't imagine how hard it must have been to be powerful enough to help, but not be able to. Still, the heartache and all the lives lost, even all these years later, it's still so devastating to think about. I feel the pain here and I didn't have to watch it firsthand." Rhys grabbed my hand and squeezed tightly. He smiled with that 'I told you so' look in his eyes. It was as if I could hear his thoughts.

"See, I told you, you're good." He leaned in and whispered into my ear.

I just smiled and nodded. I'd let him have that moment without my debating with him on just how much I'd already said and done that would disprove what his theory of my virtue. Rhys wanted to believe in the goodness that lived inside of me. He wanted to believe that my soul, my life, wasn't meant for evil. I wanted to believe it as well, that at the end of it all, once the battle was over, my life could go on in peace.

"Mom isn't home yet, but we can go inside and get some rest. She knows we're here." Rhys was now at the top of the steps. He leaned against the banister and waved us forward.

"How would she know we're here? Witches intuition? Is her place under surveillance?" I searched for cameras.

"No, I sent her a text and told her." Rhys laughed. "Believe it or not, we have kept up with current forms of communication and technology."

Maggie joined in his laughter. Well, at least they had found a common ground in making fun of me. I'd take whatever I could get as long as it stopped their bickering.

"She knows that I'm about to step foot into her house and she isn't completely freaking out?" It seemed necessary to repeat my concern just on the off chance that he hadn't been listening to me for the past few days.

"I told you, she isn't like the others." He smiled proudly and jumped down the steps to grab the bags from the trunk.

"Whatever, we have been in that car for too long and I need a nice bed to lie on. Should she get here and decide that she has switched teams, we'll just have to deal with it if it happens." Maggie skipped up the stairs and looked back at Rhys, who was struggling to carry the bags. Of course, he would try to carry them all in on one trip. I laughed as he nearly toppled over. "So, are you going to open the door or not, lover boy?"

After he finished his struggled climb to the top of the stairs, one neither of us offered to help him with, Rhys pushed the door open to reveal the quaint interior of his childhood home. I had to admit that I liked his mom's style. Nothing was overdone. Simple furnishings with sporadic splashes of color. The decoration kept in mind the level of comfort. No one could feel anything but at ease once they crossed the threshold. Plush couches and chairs and the softest of carpets, smooth and calming scents that wafted through the air.

Rhys instructed us to remove our shoes before setting foot on the carpet, and we did. Initially, I assumed this was to preserve the look of the carpet, but once we stepped onto it, I knew this wasn't the case. The fibers reached out and massaged our feet. Hundreds of tiny hands kneading and rubbing away the kinks. Maggie looked as if she would have an orgasm as she tried to walk across the floor. Her knees buckled, and she leaned on the arm of a nearby chair. Rhys laughed at her.

"Enjoying that?" He snickered more, still standing in the hall.

"Oh, shut up!" Maggie gasped in between each breath. Well, if there was any question how to get the spunky little witch in the mood, I'd bet odds that her feet were the sweet spot.

Instead of finding our rooms and unpacking our things, we all settled into the comfort of her home. Rhys took the brown armchair. Maggie laid across the red couch, lifting her feet far from the floor where the orgasmic massaging carpet could get her, and they left the matching loveseat for me. Magic was clearly at play, even without the carpet, because we all easily relaxed into our new surroundings. We said nothing else, and even my nervous concerns, the usual chatter that ran through my mind, had been hushed.

The sound of the opening door finally broke us from our relaxation. Neither of us was pleased about it, but the booming voice changed that feeling for at least one person.

"Rhys, baby!" Rhys' mother was a tall figure with curves for days. The resemblance between the two of them was uncanny. She looked too young to be his actual mother, which caused suspicion. Were her genes really that good, or had she whipped up a spell to keep her youthful appearance? I guess it wasn't too far of a stretch to think the gods of elasticity favored her. Everyone knew the old saying, black don't crack.

"Where is she?" She pushed her son to the side and scanned the room, quickly able to pinpoint me. "Ah, there she is! Just as beautiful as I had imagined her to be!"

I braced myself as the woman walked over to me. Part of me was ready to be bum rushed, knocked to the floor, and beaten. That could have been her plan all along. She wanted to corner me after having magically subdued me with the plush sofa. I told myself to keep it together as she zeroed in.

"Syrinada." My name was a statement of no doubt

in her mind of my identity. She looked at me through the eyes of a long-lost relative. Comparing the woman that now stood before her, to a child that she once knew. It made no sense to me, though.

"Yes, ma'am." I wanted to shrink myself and hide, but I stood with my shoulders back and my head high. I'd faced monsters before and won. It wouldn't be ideal considering who she was, but if a fight was necessary, there was no way in hell I would back down.

"You do not know how long I have been waiting to lay eyes on this gorgeous face of yours!" With her squeal of pent up excitement, she pulled me into an aggressively sweet hug that interrupted my breathing.

"You have?" This was not the welcome that I was expecting at all. Even with all the reassurance that Rhys had given me. Neither of us would have taken that bet that she'd be hugging me like a mama bear reunited with a lost cub.

"Oh, Lord, yes! You were just a tiny little thing the last time I saw you, not even a year old yet."

"What do you mean? You've seen me before?" She freed me from her hug, but still held me captive by the shoulders.

"Yes, just after you were born." She smiled and

touched my jaw as the happiness in her eyes turned somber. "That was the last time your mother visited me."

"You knew my mother?" My heart jumped in my chest as I realized this could be a chance to

"I did. Siliya was probably the best friend I've ever really had." She touched my chin and smiled. "There is so much for me to tell you. First things first, it is time to eat! Well, at least it's time for me to cook. You three go settle in and rest up. I'll let you know when the grub is done." She shooed us away, and the look on Rhys's face relayed to us that the best thing to do was to follow her directions without question.

"You didn't tell me that your mom knew my mom." My elbow prodded his arm as punishment for his omission.

"She asked me not to." He coughed his confession. "I'm not sure why, but it was something that she wanted to tell you herself."

"Looks like there is a lot more to this story than meets the eye." Maggie yawned. Even though we'd all spent hours in a vegetative state, she was still exhausted.

"I suppose so." Rhys smiled and raised another question in my mind.

What else was he up to? What else wasn't he telling me? It was an odd feeling to be suspicious of Rhys, but there it was. Not even the people closest to me, those who'd known me all of my life, were above deception. As he gathered the bags he'd dumped in the foyer, I watched him.

All I could do was hope that Rhys wouldn't betray me. He was the good in my life. I needed that good.

"So where do I bunk? I need a nap!" Maggie stretched her limbs after she hopped across the carpet as if it was a bed of hot coals. Rhys laughed; she would never live this down.

"Upstairs, first door on your left." He instructed, and she bounced up the stairs. "Syrinada, your room will be right next to hers. It's the second on the left, just across from my room."

"No longer sharing a bed, huh?" I asked, and he chuckled at the pout on my lips.

"Well, I never told my mom that we were, you know." he shrugged but I didn't know. What were we?

"Are you embarrassed?" I poked him. "Do you think your mother would disapprove?"

"No! Absolutely not." He lowered his voice. "I just

didn't want this to become all about that. You need to be focused on the important tasks here, and if my mother is worried about what we may or may not be doing in her house, I doubt that will be possible. She isn't against you for who you are, but she is still a mother, my mother."

"Oh. Okay, I got it." It had never occurred to me that the idea of us sleeping in the same bed might not exactly be a thrilling concept to the woman who gave him life.

It was weird, facing such a traditional consideration after everything that had happened. In a way, it was a refreshing return to normal. We all could use a little normality, even if it was the kind that kept me somewhat distant from Rhys.

JESSICA CAGE

CHAPTER 3

"*Everything looks delicious, Ms.,*" I paused; it was at that moment that I realized Rhys had never told me his mother's name. Great way to embarrass myself.

"You can call me Roxanne. It's my name." She gave Rhys the hard side eye, and I smiled, happy her disappointment wasn't directed at me.

"Roxanne, that's a beautiful name!" Maggie chimed in as she loaded her plate with food.

"It really is, and you didn't have to go through so much trouble." I looked at the large assortment of food; it seemed she had outdone herself for us.

"This is nothing. Besides, I miss having mouths to feed. It's so difficult to cook for one. I usually end up giving a ton of grub to the needy."

"Well, I'd hate to be taking food from the needy, but this is delicious. I see where Rhys gets his skills in the kitchen!" Maggie spoke around a mouth full of food. It was a true skill she had, being able to speak and not spit morsels all over the table.

"I'm glad you enjoy my cooking, Maggie." Roxanne smiled.

There were so many questions I had for her, but instead of bombarding her with my ramblings, I ate and allowed her time to catch up with Rhys. It had been over a decade since the two of them had been in the same room. I couldn't help the envy I felt as I witness their reunion. There was nothing more valuable to me, no price I could calculate that would be too high to pay if it mean I got to sit across the table from my mother and share with her the stories of my life.

There were times during their conversation when Rhys would look at me as though he knew my thoughts. The understanding in his eyes brought me comfort. My smile relayed my desire for him to enjoy those moments, regardless of how they may affect me. His happiness, their reunion, erased whatever somber feelings I had for myself. After all that happened, he deserved this moment of joy.

The dinner was filling, which made me feel the need to unbutton my jeans, which I would not do, since I'm a lady, after all. Instead, to work off the added calories, I helped to clear the table while Maggie jumped on the couch and turned on the television. Rhys went to unpack the last few items from the truck that he wasn't able to carry in during his unnecessary display of masculinity, and Roxanne finally pounced on a moment to get me alone.

"It really is so amazing to have you here. I can't tell you how many times I imagined what it would be like to meet you again and see what you looked like." She paused, leaning against the counter covered with plants, and slowly shook her head. "You are a mirror image of her, so beautiful."

"Really?" I thought of the woman in the ice. Even in her catatonic state, she was breathtaking. "Thank you."

"I wish I could have found you sooner, but that spell was mighty enough to stop me from locating you." She resumed cleaning the kitchen. "I suppose it shouldn't have surprised me. Considering how strong your Father was back then. There were very few people who could break a spell that man whipped up."

"Yeah, about all that." I placed the stack of plates in the sink and turned to look at her. "How much do you know? I mean, I have so many questions. Everyone gives me partial answers, as if telling me the entire truth will cause some irreparable break in the universe."

"Well, as luck would have it, I know most there is to know. I was there for most of it." She turned and pointed to the small parlor just outside of the kitchen, opposite the dining room. "Join me, please?"

I left the dishes in the sink, wiping away the water that spilled on the counter. Inside were two comfortable chairs, and a table already set with tea. She knew this conversation would happen long before I asked the question that led to it.

"You were there?" I picked up right where we'd left off. "What does that mean?"

"Yes, Alderic and I grew up together." She moved to pour the tea, offering me a choice of cream and sugar. After fixing her own cup, she relaxed into her seat.

"You know, you're probably the first person to use his name and not just refer to him as 'my father'." I chuckled. "It always sounds so ominous the way they speak about him."

"Well, he was my friend; at one time the two of us were inseparable until everything happened." She took a short sip from her cup. "I lost my friend long before he ever turned his back on the coven."

"You grew up together?" I straightened. "Here in New Orleans?"

"Yep, his house was just down the way from here. He was brilliant, and so carefree. All he needed was a sunny day and a glass of tea, and Alderic was happier than a worker bee in a field of flowers. That shine that you have now, that natural glow of goodness, well he had the same thing.

"Everywhere we went; it was magical, even when he wasn't casting any spells. Mystical things were drawn to him. Then his mother, your grandmother, died. She got so sick and when she left this plane to cross over to the next, she took a bit of him with her, the part of him that really lit up. I hoped it would return in time, but it didn't. It only continued to dim until it was snuffed out completely."

I listened intently as she continued to reminiscence. This was the most details I'd ever heard about Alderic. Even when I was with him, he hadn't told me much about himself outside of his love for my mother.

"When your mother came into the picture, I really thought that he changed. He seemed more like the boy I grew up with. He looked at her with adoration and even brought me to the sea with him to see her. It wasn't long until Siliya and I were having our own little meetings without him. I have to say that I am glad that we did. Who knows what would have come of this if we hadn't?"

"I wish she was still here." I ran my fingertip along

27

the rim of the teacup. "There's so much about her I wish I knew. Bad enough that I imagine her voice now. I know it's her; it has to be, although I have no way of really confirming my suspicion. Just something inside of me tells me that this voice inside my head belongs to her, but she is gone, dead, her body trapped, but her mind is gone forever."

"What do you mean?" Roxanne moved to the edge of her seat. "Siliya is trapped? Where?"

"Oh, um." I hesitated, but the cat was already out of the bag. There wasn't a chance I was going to keep it from her. "In my father's home, in his bedroom. I went in without his permission and I saw her. She's frozen. I guess he really loved her, so much he couldn't let her go, even in death."

"It is?" Roxanne perked up, as if I'd just told her she won the local lottery. I didn't know how my mother being kept as a trophy qualified as good news. "Are you sure? Frozen in ice?"

"Yes, I saw her there before we escaped. I guess it was less ice and more fluid. She was just floating there. I messed up and cracked the seal or something. That's why we had to leave. He got so angry. It was like he wanted to kill me for even having stepped foot inside of his room."

"Syrinada, I have to tell you something you may not want to believe right away, but it is the truth." She reached out and pulled my hand from the cup to hold between her own. "The premonitions that you've been having, the voices inside your head, they aren't just the workings of your imagination, child. I believe your mother is reaching out to you. I've suspected this for a while and if what you say is true, Siliya needs your help."

"My mother is dead; how could she be reaching out to me?" As far as I knew, messing with ghosts from the other side was taboo. If my mother were reaching out to me after her death, it would mean some serious magical rule breaking to reach back to her.

"You said that you saw her, didn't you? In your father's home." Roxanne asked. "She was there, not just a picture of her, but it was actually her?"

"Yes, but she was in like some weird floating crypt." I thought back to the dark room where he kept her. "It was like he magically preserved her body, that's all. You said he's powerful, right? I could feel his strength in every corner of his home. A spell like that would be easy for him to do. Right?"

"What really happened?" Roxanne looked me in the eye. "When you were in the room with her, what happened?"

"What do you mean?" I thought back. "I went in, I saw her and then, I mean, I don't know."

"Syrinada, I know this is difficult. I just need you to take a moment and remember what happened in detail." She looked me in the eye until I nodded, confirming I understood what she wanted. "You made contact, didn't you? You said you cracked the seal. How did you do that? Think about it. What did you feel while you were there?"

"I don't know. It felt like she was there with me. I know that was all just wishful thinking, though." The moment I saw my mother, I felt a connection. I wanted it to be real. If what Roxanne hinted at was true, my mother was still alive. It wouldn't be smart to get my hopes up.

"No, Syrinada, your mother is alive." Her eyes widened as she explained her theory. "I've suspected this for a long time, but I know it's true now. There is a link that exists between the two of them, your parents. As long as they're connected, their lives are one. If one should perish, so should the other. If Alderic is still alive and well, so is your mother."

"How do you know this, and if this is true, why doesn't he just wake her?" I pulled my hand from hers. "He loves her. He told me how much he did to be with her. If she is alive, why can't they just be together now?"

"I know it's true, because I'm the one that put the link there." The proud smile stretched across her face. "I was much younger, and my magic could be unstable at times. I didn't know if it would take, but I had to do something. Once I found out what your father was up to, the reason he chose her, there was no way I could stand aside and just let him destroy her."

"He wanted to destroy her?" My heart broke all over again. "Why?"

"Oh, you sweet child. I'm sorry to be the one to tell you this. Everything he told you, the stories of their great love, it's all a lie. Your mother wasn't the one who lured your father; it was quite the opposite. He chose her. He knew of her bloodline and, with the help of your aunt Noreen, they worked to create you."

"This is a lot to take in."

"I know. And I'm sorry. Your mother and I quickly became friends. I visited him one day, and I remember I was so thrilled because Siliya had just revealed to me she was pregnant with you. Though I arrived planning to congratulate him, I left with my heart aching. I overheard his plans; he was talking to Noreen about it. He thought I would join him, use my magic to strengthen his spells. I'm still not sure completely what your aunt's part in all of this was.

"Instead of a celebration, drinks, and a toast to the new wonder that would enter our lives, I learned of a deeper betrayal. The darkness I had so hoped was gone within Alderic was still very much alive and well. I didn't have the guts to tell Siliya what he had planned; I just couldn't hurt her in such a way, so I did the next best thing and cast a spell. He never knew it was I who had betrayed him. I'm sure that if he had, he'd have already taken his revenge. What I did, I know, it only fueled his hatred, and fed his evil, but I couldn't let your mother die."

"Rhys? Does he know all of this?" I looked over my shoulder as if he would appear standing behind me.

"Yes, in a way." Roxanne explained. "I only told him what he needed to know. With him going to stay with Alderic, I couldn't say too much."

"Why didn't he tell me?" There it was again, the paranoia and the suspicion. "All this time, he never said a word about it."

"When he told me you arrived there, I asked that he not say anything. You'd obviously have so many questions that he could never answer. I felt it was best if he let me give you the answers to your questions."

"He told you when I arrived?"

"I sent him there to stay with your father, hoping he would someday help to protect you. It makes those years away from him so worth it to know that he succeeded. Don't be too mad at him. I hated to do it, but I altered his memory and for a while there he didn't remember you even existed. It was necessary, though. Your father would have known if he had ulterior motives. Let's be honest, Rhys isn't the greatest actor."

"What am I supposed to do now?" I slouched in my chair. "All this just got way more complicated. And it wasn't exactly simple before."

"Fight, that is all that any of us can do can do." Roxanne stood from her seat and looked down at me. "Your father is coming and by now, he knows the role I have played in all of this. We are all targets now. We must fight."

"Wait," I stood. "If my aunt had a role in all of this with him, why couldn't he find me?"

"Also, my part to play. Your mother had a feeling thing were not right. She asked me to place the cloak on you before you were even born. Of course, I didn't deny her because I knew the truth. The moment your mother's heartbeat paused, your father lost track of you. And it works both ways. Because you were with Noreen, she couldn't find him either. Thank the ancestors she wasn't strong enough to break that barrier. I hate to say it this way, but she was stuck with you. You were lost, even to me."

"Protecting me." I huffed. "She made it seem like it was the greatest thing, so that she could be with me. So wonderful to find out now that it was really a punishment for her."

CHAPTER
4

"*What did she say?*" Maggie waited on the bed in the room assigned to me. She stretched out across the bed and tapped on the screen of her cell phone.

"In so many words, my father and my aunt plotted against my mother. He planned for me, for my creation, as if I were only an experiment." I sat on the bed next to her bouncing legs. "Their relationship was a scheme that had nothing to do with love. Roxanne believes he has something major in the works and if she's right, I'm the key to making it all happen." She met my regurgitated response with a long, silent pause. She put her phone down, sat up, and stared at me.

"Damn."

The word hung between us like a fly ready to land on a sweet treat. I'd expected more from her, more sass, more attitude, or at least a bit of witty commentary.

"My mother," I continued, might as well get it all out in the open.

"What about her?" Maggie leaned forward.

"She's alive. According to Roxanne, my mother isn't actually dead. Their lives are bound. My father and my mother. To kill one would be to kill both. If he is still alive, then so is she." I felt as if I would cry. The reality of it all, the weight of what they had kept from me. Everything that I believed as truth was once again revealed to be completely false.

"Seriously? Well, maybe we can find her." Maggie perked up, clearly ready for the next leg of our adventure. "Reunite mother and daughter. Something good can come out of this."

"That won't be hard to accomplish. I know where she is." I dropped my head into my hands and stared at my feet. All I could think of was my mother, floating, captured in ice, and it was too much to handle. My chest tightened and my head felt disconnected from the rest of me.

"Wait, you know where your mother is and you aren't with her." Maggie pushed my hand away from my face, forcing me to look at her. "Why? Why did we come here instead of going to here?"

"It's not that simple. If it were, I'd be with her now." I shook my head as if it would take away the heaviness in my heart. "She is with him. He has her inside his home. Trapping inside a case made of ice. I thought it was some sad lover's remorse. Actually, thought it was sweet. He just couldn't bear the thought of having to let her go, so he kept her there with him. That wasn't it at all. And now I know he wasn't upset that I had harmed her. He was upset that I may have awakened her."

"Wait, you think you woke her up?" Maggie stood from the bed. "Sy, you are going to have to focus your thoughts a little better. You're losing me now."

"Yes, I think I woke her. I'm not really sure. I felt her energy. It was so strong." Lifting my hands, I could still feel it. Her energy, or at least a signature of it, was still with me. "I thought I was crazy, you know. I thought I had imagined it all. Roxanne confirmed it, though. It all really happened and my mother is alive. I think she may have been reaching out to me."

"So let's go back there and get her!" Maggie jumped up. "Let's burst down the doors and rescue her. We can't let him have her!"

"You have to know it's not that simple." I stood. "He will not let us in there, and even if we got in, he's strong. That house is an extension of him. Getting in would be hell. Getting out would likely kill us."

"I didn't say that it was, but we have to try." Maggie paced in front of me. "She may be the only one who can undo all the bad that has been done."

If only it was possible for me to be so optimistic.

37

The truth was simple. There was no undoing anything. The best we could hope for was a chance at preventing something worse from happening, and there was nothing saying that my comatose mother could aid in that.

"That's a lot to ask someone who has spent the last couple of decades frozen." Even if we could get her out of there, what could we realistically expect from her? "She looks my age. Not half as old as he is. He's strong, Maggie."

"You're her daughter and you could get through to her." Maggie calmed her voice. She understood how difficult it was for me to process such dramatic revelations.

It hadn't even been an hour since I found out my mother was still alive. Part of me was fighting with the thought that I was there with her, and I left her. I could have saved her. I would have tried if I'd known she was alive.

"She's right. We have to go back." Rhys spoke. I looked over to find him leaning against the door frame.

"How long have you been listening?" I tilted my head at the eavesdropper.

"Long enough." He stepped into the room and shut the door behind him. "How are you feeling?"

"Lost, scared, and sick to my stomach." My chest

was still tight, but I fought to keep my focus because I needed to know more. "Your mom, she said she erased a lot of that stuff from your mind." He hadn't betrayed me after all; I could still trust him.

"I know." He smiled as if he knew exactly how worried about him I'd been.

"How?" I stepped towards him, eyes carrying the concern of my heart.

"She told me, after I contacted her, about coming here with you. I still don't know exactly what is going on. What I know is that you and your mother were really important to her. She went through all of this to make sure that you were okay. Tonight, I will have my memory fully restored, though I am not entirely sure what that will do. Syrinada, I am truly sorry."

"Why?" He'd been so sincere, so entirely open to me from the moment we met. "You did nothing wrong. According to your mom, only certain memories would come back to you if triggered. There was nothing you could have done differently."

"If you feel in any way that I have deceived you, or portrayed myself to be something that I am not..." he started, but I couldn't let him finish the thought.

"That is not at all what I think." I grabbed his hand and held it in mine. "If it wasn't for you, I'd still be there with him. I wouldn't have had a way to get out, and he'd be using me as an unwilling tool to bring destruction and devastation to the lives of so many innocent people."

"You wouldn't have done the things he asked." Rhys was confident in his assessment of my integrity. That gave me reason to feel hopeful again.

"Of course I wouldn't want to do it. It wouldn't be my choice to help him, but he has his ways. We've both witnessed this."

"If we are going to go try to get your mom, we need to recruit some help." Maggie rejoined the conversation. With Rhys in the role of cheering me up, it left room for her to plot.

"Help from whom?" I laughed. "Who in their right mind would willingly go there?"

"Well, as far as I know, the Denali's are still sworn to protect you." Maggie offered the obvious answer first.

"No, I will not bring them into this." I shook my head. They have suffered enough in the name of protecting me.

"Well, if not them, I have a few witchy sisters who are always down for a good fight." She pulled out her cell, ready to make the calls.

"I won't put anyone else in harm's path." I held up my hand to stop her. "We have to find another way."

"I know you don't really think that the three of us will just be able to waltz right in-and-out of dear old dad's home with no consequences." Maggie frowned as she returned her phone to her pocket.

"Rhys, what about your back door entrance?" I knew she was right, but that didn't mean that we needed to endanger anyone else. My father wouldn't let us have easy access. We just needed to outsmart him.

"I don't know if that would work. Odds are, he has already refortified his barriers. I'm not even sure if the pathways back there are still the same." Rhys shook his head. "He built most of them, and the ones that I put in place, he would have no trouble locating and disabling."

"How else are we supposed to get to her? You don't want to get any help. You only know of one other way inside. The way people talk about your father, he's already found it and turned it into a trap." Maggie was not the patient sort. Though she lacked tact, she was the open voice to my own concerns. Oddly enough, those echoes of my inner frustrations gave me inspirations.

"Wait! The wardrobe." The answer had been in front of me all along. Alderic had shown me the entrance.

"The what?" With her head cocked to the side, Maggie looked at me as if I were insane.

"He brought me in through a wardrobe, in a cabin that he said he and my mother used for their rendezvous. If we can get there, we'll be able to walk right through. I'm sure the doorway is still open." There would be no point to him closing it. Besides, there was clearly some sentimental connection that he had to the place. It was a weak point for him. I was sure of it.

"Okay, let's get to the cabin!" Maggie clapped her hands. "We have somewhere to start. Where is it?"

"On an island." I answered.

"An island?" Maggie rolled her eyes. "Let me guess, you don't know what island it is, do you? Do you even know how to get back to said island?"

"No, I don't. I was on the Naiad's walk when I got there." I shrugged. "All I remember is waking up on the shore."

"Great, so you were in some mental time warp. Looks like we've found another dead end." Maggie huffed.

Rhys must have taken eavesdropping lessons from his mother. Roxanne just outside the door in the hall. I hadn't even heard her approach. I started to ask her what she wanted, but paused when I saw the pensive expression that painted her face.

"Maybe not," she spoke up. "Your father used to talk of an island; long before he'd ever met your mother. His father had discovered it when he was a young man. He always talked about going there and building a world away from here. I think I still have the map here somewhere. He made me a copy once, told me I would be the only one he would allow to visit."

"Great!" Maggie moved to the door. "Let's see it!"

Roxanne led us to an old chest tucked away at the back of the dank basement that sat beneath her home. It was a witchy time capsule of sorts, filled with items she treasured from her childhood. She pulled out everything from her favorite skirt to a journal tied shut with twine and herbs.

"Here." She held up a wilted piece of paper.

"That's a map?" I sighed. "Of what? There is nothing on it."

"Well, it used to show an elaborate drawing. I guess the ink faded."

"Can you restore it?" Rhys asked, but his mother looked less than confident.

"I can, or I can help you do it." Maggie chimed it. "I'll just need you to tap into that memory bank of yours. I'll be able to bring it to the forefront of your mind. That way, you can recreate it. Hopefully, your drawing skills are good enough."

"You can do that?" Roxanne asked, shocked but impressed.

"One of the few useful things my mother taught me." Maggie nodded. "As long as you can get a good grasp on the memory, I'll be able to manage it."

"Great! Now we have a way in, but what exactly is

our exit strategy?" Rhys asked, and all eyes turned to me.

CHAPTER 5

That night the dream was different. It started as the same one that haunted me each night since the witch ancestors cast their judgment on me. This one felt just as real as the others had. Only I could recognize that it wasn't really a dream at all. This was the way Alderic communicated with me.

It was a mental assault. The only way he could get to me. This time, he invaded my life and filled my head with his horrible threats. He'd come for me and ripped me from the comforts of my bed.

"You will join me," my father stood at the opposite end of a large dark room. It reminded me of his bedroom, the one we would try to return to save my mother. If not for the single candle that sat at the center of the room, there would have been no light at all.

"I will never help you destroy all of those people."

I refused his claim. "What could you possibly hope to achieve by doing that?"

I had to find a way out; talking was just a way to distract him.

"I will have my revenge. It doesn't matter how long it takes." He didn't acknowledge my obvious intention to find an exit.

"Revenge for what?" I asked. As far as I knew, he was the one doing all the terrible things. He should have been hiding away, hoping that no one would seek revenge against him.

"My father!" He yelled, and the power of his voice caused the floor beneath my feet to tremble.

"Your father?" He had my attention. All of this was happening because of his want for revenge for his own father.

"Yes, the man who loved another. A vampire." His voice dropped into the darkest corner of hell as he recalled his past.

"My grandfather was in love with a vampire?" If my mouth wasn't hanging open before, it was now.

"Your mother's kind wasn't the only species that it was against the rules for witches to mingle with. Hell, anyone outside of us was off limits." Alderic continued. "After my mother's passing, my father fell in love with a vampire. He was all that I had left, and they took him from me! He tried to protect her from them and they killed him. They said she was an abomination and that he had betrayed his people by caring for her, so he deserved to die with her. They burned them both alive."

"You did all of this, tricked my mother into loving you, having me, and then killing her, and all to do what? Have your superhuman offspring destroy the world?" It was best that he not find out about my knowledge of their lifeline connection. The more I could keep to myself, the better. Alderic was way ahead in the game and I needed whatever trick up my sleeve I could get.

"What is it you want me to say?" He hadn't moved a muscle since I got there. "Clearly you're a brilliant young woman. You've surmised the gist of my plan."

"The truth! You never loved my mother, and you damn sure never cared about me. You are doing all of this to avenge your father's death, because of the hurt that was done to you." My heart broke, and I wanted to cry, but I didn't. I had to keep my strength. "Did you ever once stop to consider the fact that you are doing the same to me? Killing my mother and taking away my opportunity of growing up with a father in my life. Did that not matter to you, or are you so emotionally disconnected from your magical science project that none of this affects you?"

"You were supposed to remain with me!" His voice boomed and reverberated off the walls. As they shook, they moved in closer and forced us to decrease the distance between our positions.

I pressed my back against the wall to get as far from him as I could, but it was no use. He was so close I could feel his breath on my face.

"That doesn't answer my question!" I confronted him. "What you did was selfish and short sighted. You have to know that."

"Listen to me, child. I'm your father, and you belong with me." He chuckled. "You know; it wasn't pure luck that I found your mother. I searched for her. On some level, I loved her. I loved everything that she could give to me. I loved her because she could give me you, the child I always wanted.

"Your aunt, Noreen, she loved me. Perhaps had things been different," he drifted for a moment then returned to his declaration. "A pity she had no power. I could tell right away she didn't possess a fraction of the strength your mother held in the tip of her finger. But she proved valuable. Noreen would do just about anything to prove herself to me, even betray her own blood.

"Though it was beneficial to my plot, it actually did more to disgust me than anything. Family is everything, and she turned her back on it. Still, with my power and the power of my father linked to my own through a ritual that was banned for that very reason, I was strong and Siliya was a well of untapped magic. A magic that I transferred to you. While you were still inside of her womb, I worked my spells, and slowly over the months, I shifted her strength to you. Once you were born, I had no need for her."

"You are nothing to me!" I screamed in his face. "You're not my father!"

"How dare you talk to me like that!" Again, the walls moved inward and pushed me closer to the monster who claimed the title of my father.

"Right, wield your power. I'm stronger than you think I am. Growing stronger every day!" I boasted, to give me confidence, fake it 'til you make it. It was the truth, however. I could feel my strength growing. The more he said, the angrier I got and I felt that power building inside of me, just as it had when I was strapped to that bed. I didn't let that junky use me and I wouldn't let Alderic do it either.

"I suppose that means I ought to deal with you sooner than later." He threatened.

"Try it!" This time, it was my voice that shook the dark walls, but they didn't push in on us. Instead, it shattered. And for the first time, I saw a flash of worry in his eyes.

The rush of power that surged through my body was more than just the feeling of my natural ability growing. This power was coming from somewhere else, somewhere outside of me. Like the light of a life force passing from one of my victims, I saw it moving in ashen strands of energy. It was his power. I didn't know how or what I was doing, but it was undeniable. My father's power was moving from him and into me. It was fueling my escape, and as the world shattered, my father yelled my name. He would not be giving up. This would not be our last encounter.

I woke up again in bed, sweating and panting. I could still feel his power rippling through me. Could he tell? Did he know what I had done? My pull, it didn't just work on the mermen that I'd been intimate with. It worked on him as well. He tried to use his power on me, but I siphoned it to myself.

"Sy, are you okay?" Rhys entered the room and in two steps was next to my bed.

"Yes." I grabbed him and pulled him into the bed. I couldn't control my urges any longer. I needed him.

Experience said that he would resist me, but that was not an issue on this occasion. Our bodies hit the bed as we tossed clothing over the edge. The braid that fell at the back of my neck unraveled, and his hands twisted in the length of my hair. It didn't matter anymore, holding back from what I really wanted. I'd been so afraid of who would get hurt, and the damage it could do that I'd denied my want for him for so long. I refused to do that anymore.

"Syrinada," He moaned my name in between kisses and if he meant to make me pause, it had the complete opposite effect on me. He still did not know what it did to me when he said my name. That he didn't shorten it like everyone else did. Every syllable was another stroke of my mental stimuli.

Hungrily, I pulled him tighter into me, deepening the kiss. If he had questions, he silenced them as my hands pulled away the boxers he wore, the only thing that remained between us. He gave into me. My skin warmed more with every touch and triggered my arousal. The scent of moisture from between my legs filled the air, and he inhaled it deeply before kissing a trail from my chest down to the center of my being.

It was all I could do not to scream out in pleasure; we had to be quiet. I covered my face with a pillow and bit on the down filled cushion to muffle the sounds of my pleasure. His hands cupped my ass as he lifted me in the air. Body angled to meet his face as he moved to his knees. My mind rolled, dipped, and turned with every orgasm he coerced from me. I wanted more, and he was ready to provide it.

"Please, Rhys," I uncovered my face to see his between my legs and whispered my desperate plea.

"What do you want from me?" He asked as he kissed my inner thigh gently.

"I want you." My word coasted across heavy

breaths. "I need you, all of you."

He grinned, delighted by my response, and slowly lowered my soaked middle to his waiting erection. It would take me a moment to adjust to his size, so he filled me slowly. He was not cocky about it; instead, he took his time and enjoyed every moment of my stretching to fit him. I returned the pillow to my mouth and bit down as pleasure replaced the short-lived pain.

Slowly, his hips pushed forward against my thighs, going as far as I could take him until he retreated. He repeated this motion, slow strokes, in and out, each time reaching deeper. He watched me closely to be sure he wasn't hurting me. Once I had adjusted to him, I let him know by moving my hips, pushing back against his thrust. When I quickened my pace, he matched me. Hands clutched hold of my waist, and Rhys leaned into me.

He kissed my shoulder and moved one hand to cup my breast. His fingers teased my erect nipple, and I nearly moaned out loud, but bit down onto his shoulder to hush my cry. He growled when my teeth met his skin and quickened his pace, reaching deeper inside of me than he ever had before. It seemed my man liked things on the rough side. Because I enjoyed his reaction, the desire it unleashed, the aggression, I did it again. I bit down onto his shoulder and then ran my tongue across the impression I'd left in his flesh.

"Syrinada," He said my name, and I grabbed his

ass to encourage his release. He dug into me deeper, punched the bed, buried his face into the pillow next to my head, and with the most aggression I'd ever seen from him, he erupted.

I'd been so into him, his reaction to me, that it delayed my own orgasm. As he finished, my own began and the contraction of my walls around him caused his body to flinch.

"Damn," he laughed with a new husk to his voice. "What brought that on?"

I kissed his neck and rubbed my hand across his head. If I hadn't been so relaxed, so utterly pleased by this man, I would have reconsidered my response to his question. Alas, my mind was a mental goop, and the words fell out of my mouth. "I had a dream about my father."

"Okay, nothing weird about that at all." He sat up next to me and I laid my hand on his back.

"No, it wasn't like that." I paused, damage control. I had to make this sound less concerning. "Something happened, something I'm not sure how to explain. I need to talk to your mother." I jumped from the bed where he still sit and took to putting my clothes on.

"Okay, your dad, my mom, this conversation is making me feel really uncomfortable after what just happened here." He sat on the bed and watched me move around the room. "Can you slow down and talk to me, please?"

"Why?" I turned back to him and he looked at bit rejected. "I mean, why are you so uncomfortable?"

"I don't know; I mean, we just did something here. Something that I still think is pretty special." He chuckled. "I'd like to think that afterwards, you would be thinking about me, not our parents. It would also be nice if you weren't eagerly dressing and running away from me now."

"I'm sorry, Rhys. I didn't mean to make you feel that way. This was amazing and the fact that you were here when I needed you means more to me than you will ever understand. By the way, in case you were wondering, it was great." I smiled and blew him a kiss.

"Yeah, but now you're running off." He was right; I should have considered his feelings before hopping up and moving on to the next task as if I was just marking off another item on the 'To Do' list.

"Rhys, look, I finally feel like I am getting somewhere with all of this and when I saw you, I dropped a barrier that I've had up for a long time. It's a good thing. Okay?" I stood between his legs and pulled his head to my chest.

"Okay," He breathed me in and wrapped his arms around my waist.

"Now, where is your mom?" I asked, and he froze.

"Dammit, could you just stop bringing her up while I'm naked?" He sighed and dropped his arms. "Please hand me my pants."

I laughed. I didn't need to ask where she was. In the middle of the night, it wouldn't be difficult to find her, but the look on his face when I mentioned her was just too funny to pass up.

CHAPTER 6

"*I'm not really sure what something like this means.*" Roxanne looked at me and then back to Rhys. She knew exactly what we'd done.

Maybe Rhys was right. We should have waited to approach her. Nothing was more embarrassing than getting caught by a parent after having sex. Could she see it on my face? Maybe we still smelled like it. Whatever gave us up, she knew, and she was judging both of us.

"It means you're some bad ass power siphon. That is why everyone was so damned afraid of you!" Maggie was bouncing in her seat. She was not at all concerned about what Rhys and I had done. This was prime information for the witch.

As I watched her fail to contain her own excitement, I questioned my new friend. Why was she so excited?

Why didn't she fear me like everyone else? If there was anything worth fearing, this was it.

"Does it mean we have a chance of fighting him?" I forced myself to continue facing Roxanne.

She stood in the dining room wrapped in a plush robe and holding a coffee cup. With each sip, her eyes danced between her son and me. She looked right through us. It didn't matter that she was judging us. It didn't matter that she would likely want me out of her home; there were far more important things to be worried about. She could berate me for my violation at a later date.

"It will come in handy for sure, but only if he is unaware and only if you can actually control it. If the dream wasn't really a dream, I'd find it hard to believe that he didn't, on some level, recognize what you were doing."

"So, I'll learn to control it." I announced boldly. "I can do this."

"How? In order to gain control over it, you will need to use it. You will need to practice. How will you do that?" Rhys spoke up.

"I volunteer!" Maggie piped up and jumped from her seat.

"I don't know; it could be dangerous." Roxanne

looked at Maggie, almost as if in awe of her bravery, yet worried about it at the same time. I understood that feeling. Maggie was brave, and that was good, but would it would blind her to the dangers in front of her? Would she put herself in a bad spot because she was too eager to face uncertainty?

"Hey, we need a super-secret weapon if we are going to have any chances of saving your mom." Maggie pointed out. "I'm good, I can take it."

"She's right." Rhys spoke, and his mother gave him a look I couldn't read. "We need something that we can use against him. Even if he knows she is capable, he won't know she's mastered it. It could be just the ace we need up our sleeve."

"But what if I hurt you?" I stepped to Maggie. "You know that's a possibility, right? I can't control this yet."

"Then I just get hurt. I know you're worried about the deal you made with the coven and the spirits, but technically speaking, I am volunteering for the gig. If I get hurt, I'm the one who takes the blame, not you. Something tells me that the spirits will agree that it is best for you to learn to control this now. Wouldn't want a hiccup when you are near one of the Elders or their witch-bitch crew. If that happens, it will be the first thing they use as an excuse to take you out. We all know that's what they really want."

"I wasn't worried about the deal I made," I clarified.

"I don't want to hurt you."

"Either way, she has a point." This time, it was Roxanne who voiced her agreement. "I've seen terrible things done as a means of punishment, and that was for offenses a lot less than stealing power. That is what they will call it."

"Like my grandfather." I spoke.

"Your grandfather?" Rhys asked.

"Yes. Alderic told me about him during the dream. I asked him why he was doing all of this. Ironically enough, it would seem that all of this is for revenge. The council killed his father for loving a vampire. He did all this, spent years, decades of his life, planning out the way to get back at them." The dry laugh crossed my lips. "Imagine if he'd put that energy into being a good father."

"So, to get revenge, he figured the best way to accomplish this was to love up on another forbidden species? There is some twisted logic for you." Maggie scoffed and sat back down in her chair.

"It was a calculated decision. He knew what he was doing, what he was creating. Alderic knew all about my mom, her history, the power of her heritage. He understood what the mix of the bloodlines would create." I explained, taking a seat at the table we stood around. "I'm not the first like me, but he built his power for years and was stronger because he harnessed the strength of his father's ghost. That mixed with my mother's lineage, the power that would come should I get my stone... it was calculated. Cold, evil, and, unsettlingly genius."

"We can praise dear old dad's genius later. For now, how do we kick off this training session? We have the map, now we just need to power up our weapon." Maggie clapped her hands and peered at me like an evil genius. My father clearly wasn't the only crafty witch around.

~*~

The moment the sun came up, Maggie dragged me out to the field behind Roxanne's house. Not only was it adequately hidden, but it was far enough from the house that we wouldn't have to worry about Rhys or his mother inadvertently getting hurt. We didn't know what would happen when I actively attempted to use the power, and the last thing I needed was for Roxanne to be mad at me for stealing her power after already having had sex with her son in her home. There was only so much one woman could take.

"I'm not sure where to even begin with this." Maggie stood in front of me. Despite the danger, Maggie was the only one completely unconcerned with her own safety.

"Let's start with the basics. Explain what happened

exactly. This time, focus on how you felt when it happened." She adjusted her footing as she instructed me. "What caused the power to surge?"

"He was threatening me. He said if I wouldn't join him, then he would have to take me out before I really came into my power." I recalled the message my father told me during the dream.

"Okay, what did you feel when he said that? Were you afraid?"

"No, just angry." I corrected her. "Like I wanted to attack him, but I knew he was more powerful than me."

"Okay, that's a good place to start." She took a deep breath and stretched out her arms. "Try to channel those feelings again."

"You want me to get angry?" I frowned. "What am I? The Hulk?"

"Yes, if that's what got you to use the power the first time, that's what you'll need to tap into now. Until you can control it at will, you need a source to pull from. Your anger for your father is it."

I closed my eyes and thought of Alderic, my father, the source of my anger. It made me angry thinking about what he said and everything he did, but it wasn't enough. As I focused on his face in my mind, I expected it to come rushing forward, the feeling of power moving through me. But nothing happened.

"It's not working." I huffed, dropped my shoulders and opened my eyes to an annoyed Maggie.

"That's because you're not angry, Sy." She walked around me.

"I thought about my father like you said."

"Come on, it's there. The anger, the hurt, the pain — it's in you. Just because he isn't here doesn't mean it just goes away. Think of your life, all the years they kept you in the shadows. How many lies did you have to unlearn about who you really are? Think of the betrayal, Sy.

"He stole your mother from you. He made her believe he loved her just so she could produce his offspring. Now he wants to come in and use you to destroy countless lives! Everyone is against you; everyone thinks you're a monster!" She screamed at me and I felt it, anger and rage.

"Stop it." I warned her.

"No, come on Syrinada. You're a tough girl, right? You can take it! Big bad siren and what? Now you're going to wimp out on me? No wonder he is ready to move on. No wonder he doesn't love you!" Maggie pushed my shoulder.

"Maggie, stop."

"You aren't the daughter he wanted. I doubt you even have enough power to do what he wants! Everyone is so afraid of what you will do and you can't even face the truth! Your family is fucked up. Your aunt betrayed your mother and turned her back on you all so she could get with your dad. He tore them apart, destroyed what was likely a loving relationship between two sisters, and now here you are, years later, doing the same thing he did."

"You don't know what you're talking about."

"Don't I? They say the fruit never falls too far from the tree. The Denali's, Demetrius and poor Malachi. What did they do to deserve what you did to their relationship?"

"Stop, this isn't right." I tried to walk away, but she pushed me back to the spot she circled.

"Isn't it? When are you going to face the truth? You're the reason for so much pain and suffering. I mean, that's what he created you for. Alderic planned for you to bring nothing but pain to everyone you meet. You were born out of hate!"

"I said stop it!" I opened my eyes and Maggie stood in front of me, frozen.

A soft blue glow highlighted the edges of her body. It was her energy, her power radiating from her body. I knew what it meant because I'd seen it before, spilling from the mouths of my victims. Hoping to stop it, I lifted my hand to reach out to her, to save her, but her body lifted from the ground and a moment later, that energy that stood around her shifted away from her body. It reached for me, pooling around the tips of my outstretched hand.

I felt it caress my fingers. Tempting me, inviting me to take it in, and I wanted it. It was the look on Maggie's face, the glazed over eyes, lax jaw, and slumped body that stopped me. Seeing her that way stopped me. I pulled back from the blue glow and shut my mind to it. It wasn't right; I couldn't hurt her. She looked too vulnerable, too weak.

The blue light faded, and Maggie stumbled forward and fell to the ground.

"What happened? Why did you stop?" Maggie looked up at me.

"I can't do this to you." I tried to help her up, but she pushed my hand away. "It's not right."

"Look, either you suck it up and learn how to control this or you might as well count yourself dead." Maggie spit the hard truth at me.

"Excuse me?"

"Do you think your dad is going to sit aside and let you deal with your emotions? Do you think he is going to give two shits about how your conscience affects you? That's exactly what he's counting on happening. He is hoping that your good side will sway you. That the love you have for him, that emotional tie that exists deep down inside of you, will make you falter. That's your weak spot. He knows it and he will use it against you!"

"I just, I can't do this."

"Fine. If you want to die, then I won't fight you on it." Maggie turned to walk away from me.

I let her down. She wanted me to be stronger, to be okay with hurting her, but I couldn't. I would have called out to her, stopped her, and apologized because that's what people pleasers do. Yeah, I would have done that if she hadn't turned around and shot a ball of fire at my head. I barely dodged the flames in time.

"What the hell is wrong with you?" If it hadn't been for the training I did with Rhys, she would have taken my head off.

"What? Did that make you angry?" She shot another one at me, and I dove to the ground and rolled out of the way. "Fight back!" She screamed at me.

"You're insane!" I picked myself up. "I won't hurt you, Maggie. It's not right and you know it."

"Fight back!" She yelled again before launching another ball of fire.

I deflected her hits, each time expecting what she would do next. I skillfully avoided hit after hit. Tired of the dance, Maggie switched up her course of attack. Flames became a gust of air, not as easy to dodge. She used the current of air to crush my body. It slammed on top of me and pummeled me into the ground.

"I can't breathe!" I struggled to cry out.

"Well, stop me! Fight back! Use your power!" She ordered.

"Please, stop."

"Alderic won't stop. And neither will I!" Maggie did something then that I hadn't known she was capable of. She reached into my mind. I could feel her poking around, opening and closing doors to my memories until she found the one she wanted. When she spoke again, it wasn't her voice I heard. She'd reached into my mind and pulled out the sound of Alderic's voice. "Yes, give in. Just as I knew you would! You're weak and pathetic, not fit to be my daughter!"

That was it. I couldn't take anymore. I screamed out, a harsh sound that shook the ground beneath me. Counted out in heartbeats, everything changed. One beat. The pressure on my chest was gone. Two beats. I was back on my feet. Three beats. Maggie's body floated in the air, limp and unassuming. Four beats. Blue light pulled away from her and filled my body. It rushed into me through my eyes, ears, mouth, every opening available. I stood with my arms outstretched to the sky and cried out with satisfaction.

Maggie fell to the ground with a solid thump. I looked down at her, my thirst for her power growing. I could take more, I could take it all, drain every drop from her body. Those dark thoughts swirled through my mind for only a moment before I recognized her as my friend and not a target. Maggie was in trouble.

"Oh my god, Maggie!" I fell to my knees by her side. Her heart was barely working; her breath was shallow and wavering. "Please be okay. Please be okay."

I waved my hands over her and focused. I could do this. She would be fine. I'd done it so many times before with the plants back at Rhys' apartment. It was the same. They fed me life, and I gave it right back. I could just give it back. "Take it back." I whispered to her, but nothing happened.

"Maggie?" I heard Rhys approaching before I saw him.

"Stay back!" I lifted my hand to him. I needed to control this and having him near me wouldn't help that.

Maggie's eyes slid shut. There wasn't much more time left.

"Maggie, take your power back. Now!" I slammed my hand into her chest and felt the energy traveling up my body and pool in my palm before it found its way back to its rightful home.

Maggie's chest lifted, and she gasped as the borrowed power, her energy, leaked from my body and returned to where it belonged.

"Now, that's how you fight back!" Maggie laughed and I sighed. This girl was out of her damn mind.

CHAPTER 7

"*We have a problem.*" Maggie rushed into the dining room where Rhys and I sat together, enjoying yet another delicious meal prepared by Roxanne. Despite her urgency, we barely looked up from our plates when she entered the room.

"What is it, Maggie?" Rhys' mother stood from the table, no doubt intending to prepare a plate for the new arrival.

Maggie decided she needed to go visit her friends and family. New Orleans was home to her, but since our arrival there, she had yet to leave my side. With my new power coming to light, she felt more comfortable leaving me unguarded.

Rhys laughed and poked fun at her when she boasted about being able to leave my side. Considering who I was, he didn't think it was at all necessary for me to have a babysitter. Maggie wasn't even supposed to be around to protect me. Her objective, as described by Marlo, was to protect others from me. She was supposed to be the one reporting back to the coven if I ever stepped out of line.

"Word is out about Sy's new trick." She sat at the table ready to dig into the meal, which Roxanne hadn't placed in front of her yet.

"How is that possible?" Rhys' eyes met my own. "We have been careful, hidden. How could anyone possibly know?"

"It seems there are other spies working for the coven. Marlo had her goons out in the woods while we were there." Maggie looked at me and shook her head. "I searched that area each time we went out there. I saw no one. If you ask me, she is using a little magic loophole. If Roxanne didn't have this place so magnificently shielded, the old fart would know all there is to know about Sy."

"Dammit!" I pushed back from the table, no longer able to enjoy my meal after what I just heard. There was no way I could stop training. Honing that power was key to everything. "Okay, so what now? I need to keep practicing; I need to prepare for this."

"Now, nothing. Now it's just speculation. They have no actual proof. To be honest, most people seem to think that they are spreading rumors to stir up drama because the old hag is upset she didn't get her way. Everyone knows she wanted to take you out of the picture when she had the chance. It's actually creating a divide within the coven. A rift like this is not a good thing, but it may play in our favor."

"Their distraction buys us a bit of time, but we all know when they stop bickering, they'll investigate this further." Roxanne commented.

"You're right, they will. I think we should bring the practicing inside. If they can't get through the shield that this house is under, we need to use that to our advantage. I'll clear out the basement and you can use that for the next few days." Rhys stood from his seat and looked around the table before landing on my face. "The tide is coming soon; you'll need as much practice as you can get before then. I'm nearly finished with the map. Everything will be in place."

"He'll know that you helped us." I spoke to Roxanne. Rhys' mentioning of the map returned another nagging concern, this one for his mother.

It had been a tick in the back of my head. Alderic, my father, would know that there was only one person who could lead us to his secret place. There was only one person besides my mother who knew the way. What would he do to her as punishment for her betrayal? How would he harm her for helping me?

"There is no doubt in my mind that he will. I'm a

big girl though, and I have been waiting for this day, preparing for it. There are a few tricks up my sleeve, trust me; I can take care of myself. Besides, I think I'm safe for a bit before he turns his attention my way. At least until you all make it out of there." She sat the plate down in front of Maggie, who quickly worked to inhale every morsel. "Sy, baby girl, worry about the task at hand. Get through this one thing and then we will worry about the next."

For the next few days, it was nothing but practice. Time and time again, I pulled power into myself, stripping Maggie of her natural abilities, and just as I'd done with the plants in my room, I'd breathe it back into her. At first, it was a thrill for her, the complete feeling of void, and then the surge of power. She was having fun, enjoying the rollercoaster, but over time, it was easy to see that what I was doing was hurting her.

There were only so many times that a person could go through that. A bond stronger than blood tied magic to the soul. It was the essence of who a person was. To strip them of it, over and over, was damaging in a way that none of us could truly understand. But I saw it in her eyes, and in the color of her essence, that changed the longer we did it.

"That's enough. I can control it now." I announced after Maggie fell to her knees, gasping for air after I'd just pushed her energy back to her. This time it was different, and I wasn't even sure if she was aware of the change.

"Sy, if you need to practice, do it. I can handle it." Maggie stood up; her posture told that she was ready for anything, but her eyes told a different story. The light that used to shine so brightly was now just a dim glow.

"Maggie, we cannot keep doing this. You can't survive this." I dropped to my knee beside her.

"I told you, I want to help." She repeated the same line she had time and time again.

"And you have, but there is no way that I can live with myself knowing I hurt you so badly. That last time, it was different. It was as if I had to force your soul to accept the magic back. That can't be good." My body still tingled from remnants of her power. This was the problem; this was the fear.

Whatever was taken could never completely returned. Every time I took from her, or the plants, the world around me, no matter how quickly I tried to give it back, some of it remained behind. A part of her was now tied to me forever. It affected me, but how could I tell her that? How could I say to any of them that there was a change happening inside of me I didn't understand?

My vision shifted; the world took on a new hue, tinted at the edges with blue dust, the essence of Maggie. If her good could linger, if the beauty that came from inside of her could stay with me, what about Alderic's evil? What would happen to me when I took on that? How much of him would remain, how much of myself would I be able to hold on to?

"Look, I can handle this. I am in control now; there is no need for us to continue doing this."

"That's good to hear, because the tide is coming in. You all need to leave soon." Roxanne stood at the top of the basement stairs looking down at us. It felt like she knew. She understood my fears. She looked at Maggie and shook her head. This wasn't right, and I wasn't the only one concerned about it.

"Great, I will go tell Rhys and get my stuff together." Maggie stood up, paused for a second as she steadied herself, and then headed up the stairs.

"You see it, don't you?" I asked Roxanne as soon as Maggie was outside of hearing range.

"See what?" She looked over her shoulder, then back at me.

"Me, what I've done." I sat on the edge of the large sink used for laundry. "You see what I'm capable of."

"I see you trying, learning, struggling, and caring. That is what I see." She descended the steps. "Look, this can't be easy on you. Yes, I worry, but I have years of practice at that. There is so much to this that we don't understand and likely won't ever. As long as you hold on to the goodness inside of you, that loving heart of yours, you will be okay. I worry because I care; I am concerned because I want you to be okay."

"What if I mess up? What if I hurt them?"

"You won't." She smiled and waved me over to her. "Believe in that just as much as I do, just as much as Rhys and Maggie do."

"I struggle with that."

"I know, and you will, but in time, you will see what we do." She pulled me into her arms and hugged me with the love of a mother. I sobbed into her shoulder. "The worst thing you can do is allow others to believe in you more than you do yourself. Because then you become dependent on it, and the moment it's taken away, you crumble. Trust in yourself, understand that you are powerful."

"Thank you."

"What are you thanking me for?" She lifted my chin with her finger.

"This moment, for letting me have one moment to be vulnerable without judgment." I wiped away stray tears. "It's so hard. All of this, having to be strong, having to be a fighter. I want to fix all of this, but it is so overwhelming, and I worry about how I will handle it. How will I survive so much that I don't yet understand?"

"Listen, it's okay to have moments like this. We

all want to be superwoman and we all have her in us, but that is something that takes time. She has to be developed, nurtured, and earned. You have shown so many times that she is within you. When the time is right, your power will be there. Use it."

CHAPTER
8

Roxanne waved us off as we stood in the middle of the living room with hands connected. I hoped Maggie would stay behind, but she insisted on joining us despite her obvious need for rest. Rhys tightened his grip on my hand and nodded. I looked at Maggie, who took a deep breath and waited for the rush of magic that would transport us from the house.

We couldn't do it outside because of the risk of alerting the coven or my father of what we were planning. Now that we knew we were being watched, we had to be more careful with our actions.

The same way Rhys helped me escape Alderic's home, he took us back. Maggie and Rhys worked together, using their magic to move us across space and time to a place that existed outside of both. We couldn't get there in direct shift, so the first jump landed us on the edge of the ocean off the coast of California. The

Santa Monica beach.

I had been there once before with a friend who I met in college. She was a bubbly person who hated the water, but loved to wear bathing suits. While she posed in the sand, I purchased the coolest necklace from a guy making them along the walk. Her face came to mind, happy and carefree, and I held it there. I clung to the memory and the feeling that it gave me.

I needed to believe I could get back to that, that there could be peace in my life once again. We appeared in the middle of a crowded beach, and I froze for a moment, but relaxed when no one reacted to our arrival.

"We're cloaked." Maggie nudged my shoulder and giggled.

"I figured as much, since no one ran away screaming when two witches and a mermaid appeared."

"Well, technically, they wouldn't really be able to know that you were a mermaid." This time her giggle was it was full on laughter. The jump must have messed with her head. "So what now?"

"Now we get in." You know how you aren't aware of just how much you needed something until it's right in front of you. That moment you take a sip of cool water and suddenly you're chugging down the entire cup? The thirst was always there, but something suppresses it until you're able to quench it. That is what it felt like to have the ocean standing in front of me. To smell the salt on the air. The skin across my legs itched, ready for the transition that would allow my tail to break free.

"Yeah, that whole underwater breathing thing was never really my strong suit. Guess I should have mentioned that before." I stared at her in disbelief, how she thought any of our plans could work.

"You are something else, I swear." Rhys placed his hand over her face, and under his breath, he mouthed an incantation. "There."

"Aw, thanks lover boy! I knew you liked me. You'd never let me drown." She winked at him and blew a kiss in his direction.

"Well, you know; I aim to please." He rubbed my shoulder and smiled. "Syrinada."

That was my cue.

"Okay, but do you think you guys can refrain from bickering until we get back from our trip?" I stepped in front of them and crossed my arms. "It's only going to make this harder if I have to keep reminding you two to play nicely."

"Yeah, I'm not making any promises on that one." Maggie launched a playful punch at Rhys and he caught her fist.

"Not a single one." He laughed.

We walked into the water. Both of them gave me space once we hit a depth that would allow my legs to shift, bind into one, and emerge as a glorious red tail with golden spirals down the length of it. Beneath the water, Maggie stared at me wide eyed.

"I knew you would be gorgeous. I mean, clearly you already are, but now, I'm actually kind of speechless." She swam around me and pointed at the tip of my tail which, unlike other sirens, was pointed and now flared out. "There is just no way that I could have ever imagined."

"Thanks, Mag." I smiled, accepting the compliment.

"You really are something to admire." Rhys agreed with her. "I don't think I ever told you that."

"You have, maybe not in those specific words, but you have." Rhys moved towards me and pulled me into his arms.

"Just in case." he lowered his lips to mine and kissed me deeply. The salt of the ocean coated his lips and was an interesting contrast to the sweet taste of his tongue.

"Okay guys, enough of that. Let's do this." Maggie tapped me on the shoulder and reluctantly I pulled away from Rhys. "Just how are we going to get to the island in time?"

"Well, now it's my time to work a little magic." I smiled and grabbed her hand. I held my other out to Rhys, who grabbed hold of me.

The current moved with me. I felt it as it waited for my command. Stirring the water with my tail, I allowed my will to be known to the elements. "Hold on," I told them.

The Ocean stilled for just a moment. A nearby school of fish was suspended, held motionless as the magic built. I waited for the perfect moment when the energy was at its peak. One powerful push of my tail and the three of us shot off across the ocean.

I carried them by my side as the water rushed by us and with it all the life within. The coral, the fish, the dolphins, and even sharks who, if they were faster, would have taken a bite out of either of us.

"It's easy to forget just how powerful you are." Rhys pulled me into his arms as we climbed out of the water.

"I'll take that as a good thing." I answered, happy to have my voice back.

"Yes, please do. I just," he kissed me softly and whispered against my lips, "Damn, I am so lucky to be with you."

In the depths of his eyes, there was a look that did

both good and bad things to me. It reminded me of someone I was desperately trying to forget. His name became an echo whispered in my mind. I felt it there; it stirred deep beneath the surface in the pit of my stomach. That connection.

Once again, he was there with me and the feeling was undeniable. I shook my head, refusing to believe that what I was experiencing was real. His voice in that moment, calling my name.

"Are you okay?" Rhys asked, and I nodded as Maggie handed me the backpack that contained my clothes.

"Put some pants on." She laughed. "I mean, I know you're a badass siren and all, but it may not be so good if you're also bare ass while fighting daddy dearest."

Looking down, my eyes widened as I realized Maggie could see everything below my waistline. I turned, covering myself and took the bag, happy for the waterproofing Roxanne had done to it. Maggie was right. I wanted to find any way possible to defeat my father, but distraction by nudity wasn't on my list.

We took a moment to regroup before proceeding. I knew the way. There was no way I could forget the path that had become etched in my memory. Both times I had gone there, it appeared I had no choice. My body told me I needed to follow the path, so I did.

Though the path was the same, the surrounding forest was completely different, less abrasive, less consuming. It seemed relieved, if that was even really possible. The island was at ease, yet the closer we got to the house, the little cabin built by my father's hands, the ambiance changed. Despair. I felt sadness like a physical weight on my mind. The place itself was in mourning, but why? What had happened there?

"Shit!" Maggie blurted out as we approached our destination.

"Oh my god, what happened?" I stared at the destruction that met us.

"He knew we were coming! How could he possibly know?" Rhys bent down to the ground to assess the damage.

In front of us was the cabin burned to the ground. The surrounding earth scorched by the flames. There was no welcoming feeling, like returning home yet again. It was all gone, the wonder, the craftsmanship, it was all gone. The last thing left of my mother's memory, the one thing that still gave me hope of getting her back, was gone.

"How could he have known?" Maggie approached what used to be the porch.

"I don't know." I sighed and stood there, helpless.

"What do we do now?" Maggie, despite the destruction we met, seemed optimistic, as though there was another way. Rhys engaged in a conversation with her, but I couldn't hear the words. Instead, the voice returned to me. The one that called to me during our drive. The one Roxanne said belonged to my mother.

You have the power to undo this.

"What?" I called out and caught both of my companion's attention.

"No one said anything." Rhys looked worried. "Are you okay?"

You have the power to undo this. What is done, can be reversed.

This time I wouldn't avoid it. Instead of trying to force the voice from my mind, I listened to it.

"How?" I said aloud, which again resulted in the concerned expressions of my companions.

Look within.

"Great, of course, another riddle. Fine." I closed my eyes. The only thing I had within was the memories of the house.

I pulled those images into my mind. All of its unique details, the ingenious designs and inventions that kept the house running with a mixture of science and magic.

I chose my first night there to focus on. Thinking of the last brought anger to my heart. I couldn't take the chance that having hatred in my mind would ruin the magic I was trying to perform.

Everything from that night returned. Laughing with Verena on the couch, as we were relieved to find safety from the storm. Rummaging through the kitchen and finding drinking water inside of the magically run appliance. The bedroom in the back where my mother's locket hung inside of the wardrobe. It all came back to me. Even the rain. I could smell the rain from that first night and moments later, I felt it dripping on my flesh.

"I can't believe it." Rhys whispered his awe. I opened my eyes to find that the house, my mother's special place, had returned.

"You did that, didn't you?" He turned his eyes from the house to me.

"Yes, I believe I did." This time, my grin was a wide one. I saw a glimpse of what he'd always seen in me, that I was capable of more than just destruction.

"How?" Maggie chirped, ready for a full tutorial.

"If I could explain it, I would, but for now, we need to move. I don't know if he can sense what I've done here."

Rhys and Maggie followed me up the steps to the

door, where I paused for a moment before pushing it open. Everything was just as I remembered it. A part of me wanted to settle in and enjoy the comfort of the place my mother once loved. I wanted to look for more things that may have belonged to her, to see if there were more hidden gems, but that was not an option.

Instead of searching the place, I lead the way as we headed straight to the back of the cabin and into the bedroom that held a large bed, small writing desk dressed with an inkwell and paper, and the wardrobe that served as a doorway to Alderic's secret home. I crossed the room to the wardrobe and opened the door, but nothing happened.

"What's wrong? Why isn't it working?" I swung the door back and forward. "This is how he did it."

"Think, Syrinada." Rhys rubbed my shoulders. "What exactly did your father do when he opened the portal?"

"The back." The memory was clear. Alderic had stepped inside of the wardrobe and pressed against the back panel. Remembering this, I did the same.

I realized then that it would take more than replicating his actions to make the doorway work. I had to do something that made my skin crawl to think of. Alderic's magic lingered inside of me. I could feel it. The only way I was getting through is if I tapped into it. That bit of him, the remnants of what I pulled from him in the dream state.

It was still there and the moment my hand touched the wood of the panel; it rushed to the point of contact. Alderic's magic was his signature and the key to his defenses. That was the reason everyone else was unsuccessful in locating him. His own magic mixed with that which he borrowed from his father's spirit was unique.

I envisioned what I wanted to find on the other side of the panel, what I wanted it to reveal to me. A lush field of grass spread as far as I could see, with a tall tree line off in the distance, beyond that mountain peaks visible above the height of the branches. I pictured the house; quaint on the outside, but locked inside, was a world of infinite magic, my father's creation. Also bound within its walls was my mother.

The panel creaked and moved to the side, sliding out of view to reveal a portal of light. I reached back to grab Rhys' hand, and he took hold of Maggie as we stepped through the doorway.

The serene view that welcomed me on my first visit was no longer there. What waited for us was the hellish land that shocked me as I ran from a father who was hellbent on turning me into a monster. No longer were the grounds lush, but scorched by angry fires. The trees were bare, and the earth was sick. The smell of death was all around, and the house no longer stood as a picture of suburban perfection. Instead, we laid eyes on a house of horrors, the kind of house designed for haunted theme parks meant to frighten children.

"What the hell happened here?" Rhys said as he covered his nose. The smell of decaying flesh intensified with each step we took towards the house.

"Looks like your dad isn't huge on the upkeep." Maggie joked, but I could tell that she was worried. With her energy not fully restored, the reality of what we were walking into was finally settling in.

"It wasn't like this before." Rhys commented.

"Yes, Rhys, it was." I responded. "Remember when we were leaving? I asked you what had happened. I saw it then."

"I don't understand." He shook his head. "I lived here for so long. It wasn't like this before."

"Well, if Alderic can do even a fraction of what they're afraid of, surely he can give this place a magical facelift." I surmised as we creeped across the field. "I think that is what he did."

"This is exactly where I picture someone like him living. I mean, from what I've heard, he isn't the best of guys, and of course he would want this place to look more appealing to anyone he allowed to come." Maggie stated bluntly.

"Damn, I guess it's just hard to believe that I stayed

here all those years and never saw it."

"I don't think anyone would have if I hadn't pissed him off." I looked over at him and grabbed his hand. "It's okay."

"Do you think he knows we are here?" Maggie asked, for the first time sounding as nervous as I felt.

"There's no way in hell he didn't sense it the moment we got here." Rhys answered. "Lucky for us, it doesn't appear he's in a rush for confrontation. Let's take advantage of that."

"Translation, we're walking into a trap." Maggie huffed.

"Well, we figured that much, right?" I looked at her and she nodded.

Stepping onto the porch, the wood creaked, and slight screams of death echoed around us. Maggie stepped closer to me. The door, which was tightly secured the last time I entered, stood unlocked and ajar. A light push on the door sent it slowly swinging open. The hinges squeaked as if they hadn't moved in years. Inside, the scent of death, the stench of hatred and despair, was more concentrated than what met us on the outside.

We moved through the halls, formerly grand and magically enthralling. It was dark, small, and cold. The furniture was old, tattered, and most of it looked as though rot and decay had already claimed it. The once giggly caressing plant life, were all decayed, brown, and lifeless; as we walked by, I could feel their agony. How was it they suffered? What evil had he done in this place to cause such a reaction?

"Something isn't right," Rhys spoke.

"Yeah, I agree." I kept close to him. I didn't exactly think we would get a warm welcome home, but death and vacancy weren't the expectations either. "This shouldn't be this easy to just walk in."

"We've established this is clearly a trap, but there really isn't any chance of turning back, is there?" He responded.

"No, there isn't." I looked ahead. "There are the stairs. At least the layout of the place is the same. Alderic's room was at the top, just off to the left. We need to start there."

"Do you think that he would have kept her there?" Rhys asked. "Doesn't sound like the move he would make."

"No, I think he definitely moved her, but that is still the best place to start." I supported my decision. "It's possible I can pick up something, maybe sense her energy, and lead us to her."

We climbed the stairs slowly for fear of falling through. Each step caused a cry of alarm from the wood beneath our weight. We spaced out our approach. Rhys went first, Maggie followed, and I took up the rear. Once we were all at the top, we moved quickly to Alderic's room.

"What the hell?" Maggie asked. "Yeah, this is definitely a trap."

"Okay, we need to stop calling that out." Rhys shook his head.

The doors to Alderic's room stood in perfect condition, just as they were when I first arrived. Even though they I'd blown them off their hinges after Alderic found me inside. If nothing else, we knew we were in the right place.

"You ready?" Rhys turned to look at me as he placed his hands on the door handle. I was as ready as I was ever going to be, and there was really no point in putting it off any longer. A quick nod of my head told him to move forward. I had to face my father; I had to do whatever I could to save my mother.

JESSICA CAGE

CHAPTER 9

Instead of dark walls and windows hidden by thick black curtains, and the room that contained my mother's frozen body, stepping through the door brought us to the top of a hill where the air was clear but the energy intense. Above was a bright blue sky, and the soothing sound of a nearby waterfall echoed in the distance. We stood there, on the artificial landmark, and stared out ahead. Formed on the descending side of the hill was a staircase. Our obvious route to take.

Hundreds of stairs marked the suggested path, and they ended at the doorway to a large maze of hedges. The doors to the bedroom that no longer existed slammed behind us and when we turned to look, it was gone. Great, it was so damned predictable and so damned annoying.

"See, it's a trap." Maggie spoke and turned to Rhys as if placing blame on his shoulder. "Oh, our brave leader, tell us what do we do now?"

"I know Alderic. This is a game. If we want out, we have to play." As if punctuating his statement, a gust of wind pushed us forward, ushering our group to the top of the staircase. Maggie, small as she was, stumbled down the first few steps and landed on her ass.

"Are you serious? The big bad warlock likes to play games? Kind of weak of him, if you ask me." Maggie joked as she got to her feet again, but there was nothing to laugh about.

I had to focus. Figure out our plan before it was too late. Nothing was as simple as it appeared. It couldn't be. It looked like a peaceful place to be, and the task ahead seemed obvious. Just go through the maze, find my mom, and leave. Simple enough, but I knew there would be something much more sinister waiting for us. Alderic wouldn't let her go that easily.

"You think she's in there? Your mother?" Maggie pointed to the maze in front of us.

"Of course, she is." I looked over the field. "The question is, where?"

"I say we aim for the center. I mean, isn't that the point to mazes? Get to the center?" Maggie asked.

"I thought it was to get to the other side." Rhys added.

"Knowing my father, we're going to have to do

both if we want to survive this thing. Let's just go as quickly as we can, please." I headed down the steps, and Rhys was the first to follow.

"Standard maze, no sweat, let's go." Maggie clapped her hands loudly as she skipped down the steps behind me. Rhys mumbled something beneath his breath that I didn't catch, but when I looked over my shoulder to him, I saw the worry. Maggie could pretend things were A-Okay, but Rhys shared my fears.

Along the way, I noted everything that could be of threat. They could easily turn the thorns in the bushes that lined the stairs into daggers meant to kill. The odd patterns in the grass covered steps beneath our feet could be markings for death, step on the wrong one, and trigger an explosion or worse.

Every scenario in every action-adventure book I'd read or movie I'd ever seen was at the forefront of my mind. In the short time we were together, Alderic taught me enough to recognize danger and be wary of it. As we neared the entrance, the hedges rose gradually until they became walls of forestry that nearly blocked out the sky.

"This place is actually pretty wonderful when you think of the magic it must have taken to build all of this." Maggie spoke mostly absentmindedly as we progressed.

"Yeah, don't get too comfortable with that idea." Rhys warned.

"I agree. Of course it's beautiful here." Still in the lead, I moved as carefully as I could. "What better way to make you put your guard down than to present you with something beautiful? Relaxing. Hell, it smells like lavender here. We all know what that does."

We stopped at the small garden planted just before the arched opening to the maze. The view of roses and other wild flowers warmed my heart, but I had to shake the thoughts of peace away from my mind. Once again, it was there. That intuition, a bright red light flashing inside my mind, a warning to be careful.

"Here we go." I moved forward, my friends following me. As we rounded the first corner, my heart stopped. Ahead of us was a long stretch of pathway, no break offs. It just went on and then ended.

"What kind of maze is this? Aren't there supposed to be options, different corridors we have to choose between?" Maggie spoke as she stepped ahead of me. "It didn't look like this before. Where are we supposed to go?"

"We keep moving." Rhys spoke, and I turned to look at him. He was right; the only way we could go was forward. Behind him, the doorway was already sealing shut.

We moved along the path cautiously. As we neared the end, what was a wall with no options split into three separate pathways. Our first choice to make.

"Which way are we supposed to we go?" Maggie asked.

"I don't know. We can't split up. That is what he wants." I answered. Nothing good ever happened with the group split up in horror movies. Always best to stay together.

"Well, we better figure out something fast." Rhys pointed towards the way we'd come in. Not only was the entryway completely sealed shut, but the walls were closing in.

The branches within the hedges on either side of the pathway reached out to the others and pulled the tall forms together. The movement was slow at first, but in a moment, things sped up. There would be no time for debate. Instinct told me to go left, so I did. Rhys and Maggie followed my lead.

Just out of the corner of my eye, I could see that the path at the far right turned into a blaze of fire. I didn't see what happened to the other, but I was glad that I hadn't chosen that option. Unfortunately, our chosen path wasn't much better than the ones we had left behind.

Just after we entered, the walls repeated the same action as the path before it. Only this time, the branches shot out around us and tried to capture us inside of its closure.

"Move!" I cried as I ripped away vines that wrapped

around my leg.

We ran full speed ahead, turning only when the maze gave us no other choice, and with each directional change, we had to increase our own pace to keep ahead of the crushing threat. The walls slammed shut, emitting thunderous claps of warning echoed around us. Rhys painful cry brought me to a halt. I looked back to see him on his knees. Blood flowed freely from a large cut on his left arm.

"What happened?" I stopped. My answer came as a branch that shot out like a spear and just barely missed my head.

"Keep running!" Rhys was back to his feet. He grabbed my hand and pulled me along.

We caught up to Maggie, who stopped for no one. Finally, the end was in sight. Just ahead, the path revealed a large open field. There wasn't enough time to appreciate the relief that sight provided. The ground beneath our feet rose and the large, forested walls collapsed behind us.

Alderic, my father, was trying to crush us to death. With the final slam, we all jumped forward and hoped like hell that we'd made it clear of the sharp branches and breaking weight.

"Shit!" Maggie rolled forward, just out of the reach of vines that threatened to pull her back into their clutches.

"Are you alright?" Already I had my hands over Rhys' arm, and was working to heal his wound with my magic. I looked over Maggie's body to be sure she wasn't also in need of healing.

"Yeah, I'm more of a distance runner. The sprints are a killer." She smiled, and I actually laughed.

"What's our next move?" Rhys flexed his arm. "Good as new! Thank you."

"Are you sure you're okay? I can do more." I held my hands to his arm again but he refuse.

"Yes, I am fine." Rhys stood. "Besides, you need to keep your strength. Not give it all to me."

"What should we do now?" I looked around the field. The walls of the maze still stood ahead of us, unlike the ones behind us.

"I'm going to go out on a limb here and say that this is obviously about your instinct, not mine." Rhys pointed back to the fallen maze. "If I had chosen, we'd be burned to a crisp right now."

I thought about what he'd said. Of course, Alderic would use this as an opportunity to test me. This wasn't just a game, nor was it just part of his efforts to keep me from saving my mother from him. He wanted to see what I was truly capable of.

"My gut says to go straight through." I pointed ahead to the opening. There were five distinct pathways that lined the circular wall directly across from where we entered the field.

Each one was decorated in a flower of a different hue. The first was red, large blooms that felt welcoming, loving. Next to that, the second had blue flowers that reminded me of the ocean and, of course, lured the siren inside of me. Golden petals wreathe the third doorway and it gave me pause. It reminded me of the mountain of dust during the naiads walk. The test of greed, and the example of what it could do to a person.

The fourth was a shade of pink. Water lilies. I would know them anywhere; they were the only ones that looked familiar to me. They were my favorite, and no doubt placed there as another temptation. A distraction from my goal. If I went for comfort, I'd fail.

The fifth and final door, the one I ventured into, stood far less vibrant than the others. Sickly looking plants covered its frame. The petals were a deep purple with etchings of green and red. Even though they bloomed just as widely as the others did, they reeked of something more, Alderic's magic. His signature was all over them, more so than the others.

"Of course! Door number five, the most ominous of them all." Maggie threw her hands in the air and marched forward.

CHAPTER
10

It couldn't have been just a basic walk across the field into the already daunting looking doorway. No, that would have been too easy. Halfway across the field, the ground betrayed us. The grass reached up like hands, ready to detain us. We fought the aggressive blades off as we ran forward hopping along stoned carefully placed along our path.

The earth beneath our feet, the artificial land designed to bring comfort in a moment that inspired anything but, shifted. It wasn't just a languid slide right to left; it rose and fell, turned and flipped, and it left us to dodge the hits.

I tried to keep my eye on the doorway, our escape, but even that turned out to be a waste of time as the pathways also shuffled. Five doors lifted into the air like a game of Find the Lady that moved across the sky. I kept my eye on it, shifting my course whenever it moved, but the ground turned beneath my feet and caused my body to twist, lift from the ground, and land right on my ass.

"Stop!" I screamed out in frustration, but triggered something deeper. A blow of power exploded from within me, and everything came to a deafening halt. When everything stopped, it left us trying to regain our composure. Maggie was right next to me, but Rhys was nearly twenty feet away.

"Okay, you need to remember that trick for future occurrences. I think I am going to puke!" Maggie rolled over to her knees, dry heaved, and Rhys jogged over to us.

"Good job." He said as he pulled me to my feet. "You gonna be okay?" He asked Maggie, and she nodded between irritated coughs.

"The doors, they're all different. Where are the flowers?" The doors also stopped their shuffle and landed in the same locations, but I could tell that it wasn't right; our chosen path was repositioned as well.

"Do you think you can pick out the right one?" Maggie asked as Rhys helped her up from the ground.

"I don't know, I think so if I focus." I narrowed my gaze at the doors ahead, trying to pick up on anything that would make them easier to identify.

"Well, hopefully you figure it out soon. Something's coming!" Maggie stared at the solid wall behind us.

Rumbling sounds of heavy footfalls. Something was indeed coming for us and from the sound of repeated explosions; the wall wouldn't be enough to stop whatever it was. It sounded like a stampede, and the symphony of growls and roars confirmed it was just that. We were sitting ducks with absolutely no cover.

"I don't know, I just..." I rubbed my hands against my temples and tried to block out the noise of the approaching threat, but I couldn't. My head hurt and there was something else. Something inside of me that lingered from him. Alderic. Could he be doing this? Was he inside my head?

"Sy, calm down." Rhys stepped in front of me. Even with monsters headed for us, he was gentle. "Focus on me, nothing else. Listen to my voice. Just breathe. Can you do that for me?" I nodded. "You know which door it is. It wasn't just the appearance. You felt something when you saw it, right?"

"Yes," I confirmed. There was an emotional response to the chosen door I didn't have with the others.

"Okay, that is all you need to know. Don't look for the door, keep your eyes on me, and feel for it. Let those senses, those instincts that have saved us countless times before, let them tell you what way to go. Which one feels right?"

"Shit. Here they come!" Maggie yelled out just moments before the wall behind us shattered, sending shards of stone flying across the field.

The monsters spilled out onto the center, and they were hideous. No doubt creations of my father. Each was twice the size of Rhys. Bodies covered in an odd fur that switched between gray and red. They ran on all fours and with every howl and growl, showed rows of flesh shredding teeth. There were too many to count in the distance. Fight or flee were our only choices.

Maggie was quick into action. She used her magic, called to the earth beneath our feet, and this time used it to aid us. Walls of solid earth shot up into the air and, though they held the beasts back momentarily, it was not enough to stop them completely. The ones she couldn't block, Rhys took out with his own form of magic. He shot outbursts of energy, which knocked the beasts down and caused their bodies to explode.

"Yeah!" Maggie yelled, but stopped her celebration as we all watched in horror. The fallen monsters reemerged, but where one fell, two rose.

"How the hell are we supposed to fight beasts that won't die?" The irritated witch asked as she shot up another barrier of earth, cutting off the newly risen monsters. For now, they were all kept at bay, but we wouldn't have long.

"We aren't supposed to fight them." Understanding.

The clarity that came over me as I witnessed her distress, her anxiety. Fighting was not the answer, but neither was running away.

"What?" Maggie gawked at me. "You want to just stand here and die?"

Rhys was right; this was about my instinct, my desire, and my power. Just as I caused the earth to stop moving, that power could stop those monsters. The last of Maggie's protective barriers fell and left us once again completely exposed. Enormous beasts lunged forward, ready to finish their task.

I took a deep breath as Maggie and Rhys took off running. I stood firm and stared at the beasts who charged us. Instinct told me to call to them, to feed them my song, and I did. The moment the melody passed my lips, their movement ceased. Large, aggressive, fearsome creatures stood before me with puppy dog eyes. Their bodies swayed to my song and as I continued, their forms became less imposing. The longer they listened, the smaller they became.

"How are you doing that?" Rhys asked, returning to my side.

I didn't answer; I just continued to sing. In my siren voice, in the melody of my song, I asked the creations of my father to show us the way. Each one knelt slowly to the ground with their noses pointed at the right passage. The choice was the right one. I could feel it as the power of Alderic that still existed inside of me swirled in an expression of its happiness, as if it recognized what was there.

"This way." I turned to the door they showed me and started walking.

"How can you be sure?" Maggie asked, wary of my choice.

"Because I'm listening to my instincts like you said." I looked over my shoulder at her dirt stained face. "This is all clearly a test, puzzles for me to solve. Well, I'm doing it, and this is the way."

Rhys didn't question me at all. When I walked, he turned to follow me and eventually, with some hesitation, so did Maggie.

I stopped just outside the door and took a deep breath, checking my gut. This was it. I'd chosen correctly. I reached out to open it, but it did the work for me. On the other side, I could see nothing, no hint of what awaited. I had to step out on faith.

We passed through the opening into the void, still unable to see what was there. Just as before, the view cleared, as if marking the finality of the choice. The door closed behind us and vanished. There was no turning back. First the sky appeared, clear and vast, and then the field. Green grass, a few trees, nothing astonishing at all, but it felt safe. For the moment.

"How did you know it would work?" Maggie spoke in between deep breaths. "How did you know that your song would affect them?"

"I didn't know for sure. Something inside told me to try it, so I did."

"Why didn't it work on us?" She looked at Rhys this time for an answer. "I mean, aren't those songs supposed to be hypnotic to anyone who hears it?"

"I have learned to control that side of myself." I answered the question Rhys had no answer to. "If I want, I can direct one person at a time or many. It was something I had to learn fast."

"It's good; you're listening to your instincts more. You're also becoming more comfortable with your power. This may be an odd time to say this, but I'm proud of you." Rhys smiled and pulled me into his arms for an impromptu hug.

"Thank you," I gave in to his hug and let the moment last as long as it could. We weren't done with our task yet. We still needed to find my mother and our way back home.

"I'm truly impressed. I worried you wouldn't figure that out." Alderic's voice rang out above us. In the sky, a projected form descended to the ground. If it weren't for the static look, I'd have thought it was really him. "Moving ahead will not be so easy, my dear child."

"We can take on whatever you throw at us!" Maggie spoke for me, but I just looked on. He wasn't here to have a conversation; he was here to deliver a message.

"And I will have the pleasure of watching, but just in case my daughter here is having any second thoughts about proceeding," He waved his arm and a forested wall appeared to the left of us. It split open to reveal a path that led back up the hill to where the door to his bedroom stood. "Now is the time to turn back. I will offer this option only once."

"There is no way that I'm leaving here before I get what I came for!" I called out.

He couldn't have possibly believed that it would be so easy to get me to turn away from the chance of saving my mother. I'd taken on everything he had thrown at us and survived. I was close. He wouldn't have bothered to come if I wasn't.

"Very well. Have it your way." He smiled, holding an unsettling and longing look for me. Alderic waited for me to backtrack, but when I didn't, he disappeared.

"If he wants us out, why doesn't he just come kick us out?" Maggie pointed to the wall that closed before more appeared, creating a new maze in front of us.

"Alderic isn't a fool, Maggie. He knows Syrinada is different, stronger, and he is testing her." Rhys pointed to the new maze in front of us. "He carefully designed all of this so he could learn more about her. He is trying to see just how much she has grown into her power."

"Sy, you can't play into this. You can't let him know what you can really do." Maggie lowered her voice as if Alderic wouldn't hear her if she whispered. This was his world.

She was right, though. We needed that secret weapon, my ability to steal his power to remain a secret for as long as possible. Even if he knew I could do it, he didn't know that I had been practicing, and that I could control it. It was in our best interest to keep it him in the dark.

"Yeah, I know; not unless I have to. I'm trying my best not to." I agreed with her.

"What do you mean?" Rhys asked, looking into my eyes. "Are you okay?"

"Can't you feel it? The intensity of the energy here. He forged every inch of this place with his power." I'd been blocking it out, but the further we went into the maze, the stronger it got. Alderic's magic was literally dripping from every branch, discolored flower, and atrocious beast we encountered.

"I feel nothing besides the pain in my ass from falling on it so much." Maggie answered. "Rhys? Do you?"

"I can tell there is some serious magic going on in

here." He shook his head no. "It's nothing like what you're saying, Syrinada."

"Look, we need to keep moving. We can't be that far away." I turned my attention to the puzzle in front of us. How would we get through?

There was no point in explaining what I felt. They wouldn't be able to understand it, anyway. Besides, I didn't want to have to be the one to explain it. I also didn't want to have to admit that Alderic's magic, his dark power, was still clinging to something inside of me and no matter how many times I tried to dispel it, it held on.

My father was evil, but there was more inside of me that the remnants of his darkness. There was goodness, peace; there was the power that only the love of a mother could produce. The closer I got to her, the more of it I felt, and the better I felt. Beneath the layers of his hatred and contempt, she was there.

She was alive, and she knew I was coming for her. My mother, she'd been with me all along. I just needed to reach out to her. To feel her as I had Alderic.

"Please, guide me." I thought to myself, directing my thoughts to the voice I'd heard before. "I know it's you, mom. Please, lead me to you. Let me save you."

"Syrinada." The voice was there again, calling my name.

"It is you, isn't it?" I spoke out loud when the voice responded.

"Yes." I could hear the smile in her voice, my mother.

"Help me find you. Please, show me the way." I asked.

"This way." In front of my feet, the path lit up. Small lights like that of fairies dusted the ground and shot off into the direction of my mother. I followed the clue that only I could see and motioned for my friends to follow.

"How can you be sure?" Maggie, now the constant skeptic, asked.

"Just trust me. This is the way."

"Let her do this." Rhys said gently to Maggie, and I smiled. He always believed in me so completely.

I continued walking because no amount of doubt could make me turn away from the path. It was definitely her, and I knew it. Alderic couldn't possibly fake that kind of goodness. The light provided by my mother's energy led me to her.

But even with her help, we had to be mindful of every move we took. Being on the right path doesn't mean your journey will be free of obstacles. Alderic wouldn't allow it to be that simple. Understanding how his mind worked left us all on edge. One wrong move, and any of us could be lost for good. As soon as the thought of our wavering safety crossed my mind, the artificial environment proved my point.

The tumultuous sound was confusing at first. We were in a field, yet it sounded like the waves of the ocean crashing around us. It was impossible. Or so I thought. Moments later, I saw the peak of a giant wave reach up in the distance. It rushed for us and there was nothing we could do but brace for impact.

It wasn't just one wave; the sounds echoed from every direction. He had us trapped.

"Rhys, cover your faces." I instructed him and he quickly worked his magic to allow both himself and Maggie the ability to breathe underwater yet again.

All I could do was prepare myself for what was to come. This wouldn't be a normal flow of water. We could survive, even if we got a little beat up. I turned in time to see the biggest of the threatening flow. Coming from behind us was an enormous wave, big enough to eliminate all views of the artificial sky.

A closer look revealed that there was so much more to his plot. He knew that water wouldn't hurt two witches and a siren. The water would barely faze us. Inside the wave, being carried along in the waves, was a familiar form.

I followed the outline of the large tentacles, past the massive body, to a set of eyes that recognized me just as I had them. My father called a monster, a beast that haunted the tales of pirates; a creature who I once believed was just a product of imagination.

The Kraken.

CHAPTER
II

"**You have got to be kidding me!**" Maggie spoke, and the wave reached its peak.

"Brace yourself!" Rhys yelled, and we all scrambled to find something to grab hold of, but of course there was nothing. Moments later, the wave crashed against the ground and sent thousands of gallons of water our way. The impact flung our bodies and both my partners went in two separate directions.

My tail emerged and though I wanted to find them and be sure that they were all right, there was no time to waste. The best way to save them was to protect them from what was coming. I was the intended target, the focal point, but it would seem the Kraken was adept at multitasking.

Though it swam toward me, its arms reached out in either direction. I did not know where Rhys and Maggie were, but it did. There was nothing else I could do but fight, and so I did. I charged straight ahead and looked the beast directly in the eyes as I did.

This creature had my number. It certainly hadn't forgotten the pain I'd inflicted on it with the use of my tail when I'd first encountered it. The damn thing tried to take out my guide, and I wasn't allowing that to happen. This time, it was prepared and its tentacle wrapped, suction cups and all, around the length of my tail.

No matter how I tried, I couldn't free myself, and struggling only seemed to make it worse. There was one moment of panic, just one, before I regained myself. This would not be enough to stop me from succeeding. My call wouldn't be enough to distract it; I needed something more. My siren song would not easily sway this thing that was told to only listen to gods. There had to be something more I could do, some way I could fight it.

I relaxed my body, which proved difficult considering the painful position I was in. Struggling made the suctions tighten and the scales of my tail peeled away. Each time another one was ripped from me, I screamed out. There was another way. There had to be. This was just another task, another puzzle to solve.

My body could heal quickly while submerged in the water. It was the only thing that kept me from passing out, the feeling of the cool fluid moving across my skin, the energy it fed me. That was my solution! That was the ticket out! The water, there was so much power in the currents; so much magic that flowed within the movement. Silently, I asked the water to fuel me, to give me the strength needed to defeat yet another monster.

The first pulse was barely enough to cause a ripple in the water, but judging by the quiver of the tentacle wrapped around me, I knew I was on the right path. Again, I called the water to aid my cause. Emitting my Siren's call not through my mouth, but through my entire body like a sonic wave. The pulsation spread through the waters and commanded that it do as I ask.

The water amplified my voice, silent, but strong. Again, the ripple spread, underwater currents that pushed against the beast. First, it was confused. Unsure what the feeling was. As my influence strengthened, it was in pain. It screamed out and retracted into itself. I pushed the pulse over and over until the tight grip around my waist lessened and I could swim freely.

Once clear of its grasp, I called to the power that I had become so familiar with and focused on the amplified call. The water would do as I asked, and this time I had a different plan. Instead of using the water to inflict pain, I asked that it retreat, but only from concentrated areas. The Kraken needed the water more than anything else. So I took it away.

A pocket of air formed around the beast, and it fought to get back to the water. The air was cruel and artificial. It likely could survive outside of water, but Alderic built his world with evil intentions that worked against the beast he brought to hurt me.

With each struggled reach, the life drained from it. I didn't want to kill it; I couldn't be that evil. This thing was following the terrible command of my father. It didn't want to harm me, or so I'd hoped. Just as the last flicker of light drained from its enormous eyes, I released my hold on the water and allowed the beast to reclaim its home.

Terrified, it quickly retreated. The water drained from the maze, leaving me standing alone. I still lost Rhys and Maggie, and without the ability to swim to higher ground, I could not easily spot them.

"Please, show them the way." I asked of my mother.

"I will." She responded softly.

I hoped like hell that it would work and that they could see the path and that they wouldn't think it was one of my father's tricks and go in the opposite direction. Time to time I would hear screams, Maggie, she was okay, she had to be. I heard Rhys' battle cry and growls of beasts. He was strong; I knew he could protect himself.

Nothing attacked me, nothing sought to harm me. This was now my punishment, my torment, listening to my friend's agony while being able to do nothing to help as I ran to my mother. My father was a sick man.

When I made it to the center of the maze, Maggie was there, knelt down on the ground. Rhys was not. The trail of light that told me where to go was gone and in the center of the grounds was my mother, still encased in the watery prison.

"Are you okay?" I ran to Maggie to make sure she was not harmed.

"Yes, tired and sore, but I will survive. Where is Rhys?" She held her shoulder and I could see that something had dislocated it.

"I don't know; we were all split up." I moved her hand from her shoulder and placed a firm hold there. "Brace," I said simply, before jamming her shoulder back into place.

"Shit, we need to go look for him." Maggie said after a series of curses beneath her breath.

"No, I'm fine, I'm here." Rhys stumbled through the path the exact opposite from where I entered the green center. He was bleeding, his shirt stained with his own blood.

"Oh, my god! What happened?" I ran to him.

"I guess I just wasn't as quick as I thought." He laughed and cringed.

"We need to get you home. This place, I am so sorry." I worked to heal him, but I was tired and my magic drained. There was little I could do for him.

"Sy, this was important. I will be fine," he pushed my hands from his injuries. "Your mother is our concern now."

"About that. How do we get her out?" Maggie, who had apparently run after me, asked and turned away from us to stare at the center of the field.

My mother was there, trapped in the encasement that still had the crack I caused when I first saw her. The weeds had grown to cover her and flowers bloomed around her. It was magical, beautiful and yet heart wrenching. She deserved to be free.

Nearing my mother, I held my breath, hoping that this wasn't just an illusion, that it wasn't another sick game my father had played. He couldn't take her from me, not after all that I had gone through to get to her. In the distance, I could still hear the sounds of threats echoing, growls, rushing waters, and battle cries. In front of me, my focus, my mother waited for me to free her. I stepped cautiously, aware of the traps that may lie ahead. I made it to her easily. No harm came.

This time was different. I could feel her energy as it radiated around me. It became warmer the closer I got. My mother was welcoming me home. She was my home, the only one I had, and finally I could return to her.

This time, there was no doubt about my action. I knew what I had to do. The thing about accepting the power inside of me was also accepting the naturalness of it. All I had to do was clear my mind. I touched the glass, placing my hand in the same spot as before.

With everything in me, I reached through it. The glass returned to the same shimmery cell of water that it was the very first time I saw it, and my hand passed right through it to grab the hand of my mother for the first time. Her eyes opened, and I heard my mother say my name. Not an echo in my mind, an eerie ghost of her voice, but I saw her lips form to say the name she'd given me at birth.

"Syrinada." The surrounding water fell away and my mother fell into my arms.

"Mom," I smiled as I struggled to hold on to her.

Rhys was there to lift her, knowing I could not hold her weight on my own for much longer.

"Good job, daughter." Alderic's voice amplified across the field.

"You stay away from her!" I yelled out. He was still nowhere to be seen, but I could feel his presence there, the darkness of his spirit.

"It is not her I want," he bellowed. "It is you. It has

always been you, child."

"You can't have either of us!" I screamed out. "You don't deserve us!"

"And just how do you plan on stopping me now that you have come into my world? There is no leaving." He materialized just a few feet away from us. Dressed head to toe in black with his hair pulled back from his face. This time, it was really him. He stood with his hands behind his back. "You will never leave here, none of you!"

"You can't keep us here." Maggie boasted as she stepped to my side opposite Rhys, who held my mother

"Well, that is where we must agree to disagree. I think I definitely can keep you here. I am stronger, smarter, and this is the world that I designed. Just how do you think you're going to escape it?"

"By kicking your ass!" Maggie boasted.

Alderic held his hand up to her; he did not move a step in her direction. "Silence, child." With those two words, Maggie's body fell to the ground. Her head smacked against the surface hard enough to echo throughout the space. Suddenly my father's creation, his world, went silent.

"Maggie!" I yelled and ran to her side. "You didn't have to hurt her!" I screamed at my father.

"I'm sorry, but she threatened me, and in my own home." He shrugged as if Maggie was no more than a fly he swatted away from his ear. "Someone should really teach that child some lessons in manners."

"You're out of your mind." Rhys spit.

"You. The betrayer, you have no right to speak to me. I taught you everything. Raised you up for that bitch of a mother who sent you to me. Now, here you are, twisting the knife that you already plunged so deep into my back. What should stop me from ending your existence right this moment?"

"You will not harm him, or anyone else!" I stood now, tired of him threatening and hurting the people I loved.

"Once again I ask, and who is going to stop me?" He tilted his head to the side, a snobbish way of punctuating his thought.

"I am!" I stepped from Maggie; she was still breathing, still alive. We had to get out of there, and the only exit was through Alderic.

"Great, well, let's just see you try." He held his hand out, beckoning me forward. "Come on, my daughter; hit me with your best!"

I accepted his challenge and centered myself. I needed to be clear of mind. He stood, an amused grin on his face and, just like before in my dream, I pushed my power at him. That wiped the smug look from his face as the blast nearly landed him on his ass. He readjusted himself and sucked his teeth.

He toyed with me before, but now, papa was mad.

Without a word, he flicked his wrist, sending a gust of wind that knocked me down. I jumped back to my feet immediately and prepared for my next move. Again and again, we exchanged blows. He hit me with air, fire, earth. Each controlled element pounded my body, but I wouldn't give up. He made his mistake. From the waterfalls that appeared in the distance, he called in a flood, but water was my element.

The water rained down on us, but not a drop touched any of us. Instead, it shot at Alderic. This time, instead of calling the water to evacuate, I shoved pound after pound of the rushing fluid into the small pocket and it worked to crush my father. His eyes bulged and his hands clawed at his neck as he struggled to hold on to the last bit of air in his lungs last.

It was not enough; he combated my efforts. Instead of holding on to that air, he used it to his advantage. The small bit of air he pushed from his lips collected around his face, then pulled the oxygen through the watery cell until it expanded enough to disrupt my own force. With a loud pop, the water burst and fell to the ground in a puddle around his feet.

"Enough! This will end now!" Alderic yelled.

I wanted to hold back, but there was no other choice. I was weakening, and I knew he could tell. He pushed harder at me until I had nothing left to fight back with.

"You are my design and you will do what I created you for!" He commanded.

"You'll have to kill me first." I defied him, then dropped my head back.

I breathed in and pulled in the power that lived within him. It came not only from the man that stood in front of me, but from the world he'd crafted using the magic. I absorbed the energy until my body floated from the ground. When my head lifted, I found my father staring at me in horror.

When our eyes re-connected, I could tell that he knew. If there was any doubt before, it was gone now. The cat was out of the bag. This distraction, his awe at this power I possessed, was just what I needed to get us out of there.

In an act of desperation, I pushed that stolen power back at him. I knew it would overwhelm him long enough for us to get out. With some of the lingering magic, I created a portal, a doorway to freedom. I grabbed Maggie and Rhys carried my mother through a free standing door.

I shut it tightly behind us and erased the connection. I looked at the closed door and felt victorious, but when I turned around, proud of what I had accomplished, everything was wrong.

CHAPTER
12

"*Where are we?*" I held on to my mother's hand who stood by my side. Rhys was no longer there. Neither was Maggie, who I was more concerned for.

The blow from Alderic had seriously injured her. And that was after she'd already taken on so much physical abuse. Combined with her having let me practice my magic on her, Maggie was way too vulnerable. Rhys was with her. I told myself he would take care of her. I had to believe that he would keep her safe until I found my way back to them.

"I don't know." She looked over her shoulder as if afraid my father would be there.

Could this be another one of his tricks? Had he made me believe I had the power to escape him, only to deceive me into letting him separate me from my friends?

The familiar feeling the room gave me told me that wasn't the case. Alderic had not created this place. It felt much like the naiads walk. Everything seemed so real, yet in the back of my mind, I knew it was more an illusion than reality.

Was this another test? Were the coven's ancestors punishing for waking my mother? Was it penance for betraying my oath to be bonded to Demetrius? I'd messed up in so many ways, and the whole point of everything I was going through was to prove that I could lead my life without faults. What would be the punishment for not living up to that?

The room was bare, void of color and any memorable characteristics. White walls that held no markings stood at our sides and back. The only thing that stood out was a single black door positioned directly ahead of us.

"We have to go through." I spoke, and she nodded her agreement. Being that there was no other option, it was clearly the way we had to go.

Together, hands still bonded between us as we stepped forward, we passed through the door and on the other side was another room. This time it was smaller and filled with decorations that fit a nursery. It was a narrow space that felt much bigger than the square footage presented to us. The feeling of love was so substantial that my heart warmed and I cried.

Whoever occupied the space had filled the room. It wasn't just the inanimate objects positioned around the room that made it feel so welcoming. They bathed each nook and cranny with their love. In the corner sat a small purple bassinet with gold and pink swirling patterns. My mother gasped, obviously recognizing where we were.

She walked over to it, letting go of my hand to touch the fabric that lined the inside. The wood frame, where there was no coloring, had small carvings, the tails of sirens.

"Where are we?" I asked her. She knew the answer, even though I hadn't put it together yet.

"I haven't been here in so long." She choked on the words.

"Where is here?" I asked again softly. She was struggling, and I wouldn't add any anxiety to what she was already feeling.

"Your nursery. We were only here for a short while before we had to run, before the covens came for us." She lifted the faded blanket to her face and inhaled a scent that I knew was more memory than actual fragrance.

"This is where we lived?" I picked up a small glass figurine from the dresser.

"Yes, your father and I built this place together,

forged with our magic. It should have been strong enough to keep you safe, to protect our family, but it wasn't." She sighed, placing the blanket back down. "Something went wrong."

"Noreen, she betrayed you." I spoke about my aunt and her sister.

"Yes, I know now." She ran her hand along the side of the bassinet and faced me with sorrow filled eyes.

"You do?" I frowned. If she knew, why didn't she protect herself?

"Yes, after your father suspended my life, just before I lost consciousness, I saw the two of them together." Her eyes flooded with unshed tears as she spoke. "She held you in her arms. He kissed her, and I wanted nothing more than to take you back. At that moment, I saw every mistake I had ever made. I witnessed the fool that I had truly allowed myself to become."

"There was no way that you could have known."

"Your aunt, my sister, she always despised me. She hated I had such an obvious talent of power, but never attempted the naiads walk. Not a day went by that she didn't bring up the topic or try to convince me to take on the challenge. To her, it was unfair. I never understood how she could blame me because she tried and failed. I still am not sure."

"Why didn't you try?" I asked, curious myself. If she had, she would have been able to protect herself.

"I didn't want it. I didn't want the power or the responsibility. What I wanted was you, a family. I wanted to be loved and to share the love that I held inside of me. That was what was important to me. Not power, not revenge. Noreen," she shook her head, "my sister always wanted to exact some vengeful fight against the covens for what they had done to our people.

"She was weak. Her power never presented even without the stone, and everyone could tell she did not possess the talents necessary to take on witches, so no one listened to her. I always believed that her blackened heart made her that way. We shared the same bloodline. There was no reason she should not have had the same access as I had. The power she wanted so much was inside her, but because she was so blinded by hate, she could never reach it."

"To think that the two of them were so much alike. Alderic and Noreen both wanted revenge for things done to those before them. Both wanted power. Unfortunately, she got the short end of the stick." In a sick and twisted way, they may have been the ones meant to be together.

"She played her part." My mother rejected my sentiment that Noreen may have been wronged. "Her choices were her own. No one forced her to betray us."

"Do you hate her for what she did to you?"

"I should, but I don't. Whether or not I hate her doesn't absolve her of the evil she's done. He likely fooled her, just as he did me. I thought he was truly in love with me, that he wanted all the same things as I did." She looked around the room where she planned to raise me. "I was just a tool, a pawn in his game, and so was she. He knew what we wanted, and he promised both of us the very things that we dreamed of. I cannot be angry with her for chasing her dreams. I just wish it wasn't at my expense, or yours."

"That is wise of you, Siliya. Our sisters are often the ones to bring us the most pain, even though they may not always intend to do so." The small ghostly voice, one I had heard before, spoke from behind us. I turned to see a familiar face.

"It's you." I looked at her and felt relieved. Of all the ghosts to appear, she was the one I would most care to have a visit with.

"Yes, I'm here to help." She stated simply, then fiddled with a small toy on a nearby stand.

"Help? Why?" I asked the young girl dressed in a simple white dress that stood in sharp contrast to her dark brown skin.

"Your father." She looked up at me with eyes full of the moon. "He is wielding some ugly magic and if he gets to you, you will help him."

"I would never!" I rejected her idea. There was no way I was going to help him hurt so many people.

"Unfortunately, the choice will not be yours to make. Now that you have pulled more of his magic into you. Doing so has left you much more vulnerable to him. He is strong enough to control that ability if given the chance. You will need all the help you can to resist him."

"What do you mean?" I asked.

"I mean; your father knew exactly what you were capable of, Syrinada. It is the entire reason you exist. To absorb the powers of others. Today, you proved his theory to be correct. He allowed you to take from him because he needed you to. Now, there is a piece of him that remains inside of you, like all of your victims. Alderic just installed a bomb within you and you can bet your tail it's counting down."

"Ebon, I can fight it!" I looked between her and my mother, who looked like she was about to cry. "I'm strong enough to fight him."

"Perhaps, but perhaps not." the ghostly girl pondered. "If not, I will be there to help."

"How are you supposed to help if I am some puppet?" I challenged her. What if she wasn't strong enough? "And why would you want to help?"

"If it comes to it, I will give you some of my power willingly. From within, I can fight him. And I must, because if your father gets his wish, he will unleash hell on earth."

"What?" My mother stepped forward. "I thought he just wanted to get back at the coven for what they did to him."

"That may have been his plan in the beginning, but plans change. Alderic hopes to bring his father back from the other side. To do that, he will need to open the door to the afterlife, and when he does, your grandfather will not be the only one to come through." Ebon sighed. "The spirits are all waiting for it to happen. They feel it, but there are some ugly things on the other side of that door. Things that we cannot allow to break free."

"Is any of that actually possible?" My mom looked at the girl with fear in her eyes.

"If it weren't, I wouldn't be here." She shrugged. "I am dead, after all. I have a lot of other things I could do. For instance, I could be watching my descendant who has her dance recital right now. The girl has two left feet, but she gives it her all."

"What now?" I asked, feeling discouraged. "How do we stop him if it's too dangerous for me to get close to him?"

"Now, you use your power on me. Pull my energy into yourself." She placed her hands on my shoulders.

I looked down at the innocent face with eyes that had seen more than I could ever know. With a deep inhale, I did as she advised. I pulled the power of a centuries' old witch into me and it was nothing like ever before.

The power hummed through my body, lighting me up from within. My hair flowed around me and I lifted from the ground and floated as if submerged in water. Her hands fell away, and she stared at me with a smile on her face.

"You, my child, are truly going to change the world."

Ebon's words were an eerie echo around us as the ghostly realm faded away. I quickly reached out to grab hold of my mother's hand. I would not lose her again.

CHAPTER 13

I stood outside the home of a powerful witch with my siren mother and a centuries' old ghost. What an awesome trio. "How long has it been?" I looked at Ebon for the answer.

"Just a few hours." At least that meant we wouldn't be walking into some flash to the future.

As I made it to the top step, the door burst open. Roxanne ran forward and pulled me into her arms. "Oh, thank goodness you're okay. I couldn't imagine losing you again. Your mother would never forgive me!"

"Yes, I'm okay, I promise." She squeezed me tighter, then her arms relaxed, and I knew she laid eyes on the figure behind me.

"Siliya?" She let me go and gently moved me to the side. "It's you; you look exactly the same as when I last saw you." The two embraced, and my mother beamed.

"Roxanne, how I have missed you!" Her voice shook with a telling blend of delight and sorrow.

"Oh, Siliya, you're here!" Roxanne repeated the statement as if repetition made it more fact than fiction.

I understood her motive. With all that was going on, I felt the need to pinch myself from time to time just to make sure I wasn't dreaming. My mother was back, and my father was after me. Was this a dream or a nightmare?

"Yes, I'm here. It's so good to see you again." They continued to hold on to each other like long-lost sisters. "My friend, thank you."

"What could you possibly have to thank me for? I feel like I failed you, all this time lost." Their hug ended and Roxanne's shoulders dropped, ashamed that she hadn't been able to do more.

"You kept my daughter safe, and you tied my life to his so that I could be here for her now. He would have done much worse to me had it not been for that link between us. You did more than anyone could have ever asked of you. That is something that I'll never be able to repay you for."

"I just wanted you to be okay." Roxanne wiped tears from her eyes, "I couldn't believe that Alderic, my friend, could do something so terrible. It was my responsibility to do everything I could think of to protect you." Roxanne looked at me. "Both of you."

"I'm okay now." My mother smiled and hugged her friend again.

"Look at you! It's like you haven't aged a day in all these years!" Roxanne held my mother at arm's length and repeated her earlier sentiment. "How is this even possible? They say black don't crack, but tell that to my crow's feet. What's your secret?"

"Well, that is a perk of being a siren trapped in waters from the sea." she explained. "We don't age as quickly as long as we are underwater. He kept my body suspended in the water from my home."

"Well, I'm just glad to have you back, even if I look like an old hag standing next to you." The two of them laughed.

It felt so good to hear my mother's laughter. Even better to see and feel the happiness she was experiencing. Every time she laughed, smiled, and hugged Roxanne, I felt a wave of joy wash over me. It wasn't my own. My mother's power was strong enough to impact those around her with her own emotions. No wonder my aunt's jealousy drove her to betrayal.

"Where is Rhys?" I didn't want to interrupt their reunion, but I had one of my own to consider.

"Oh, he is with the girl." Mournful eyes met my

own and my stomach dropped. "Maggie, she isn't doing so well."

"What?" It didn't make sense. Rhys would have undoubtedly worked his magic to heal her, so why was she still suffering? What went wrong?

"Your dad did a serious number on her. I'm not sure how or if she will come through this."

"How could I have forgotten? She hit her head when she fell. I just assumed that she would be okay. Where are they?" For the moment that she had left my mind and her pain, I felt immense guilt. Maggie was under my watch. She was there to help me, and yet I'd let her down.

"Upstairs, in her bedroom." Roxanne directed me.

The stale air inside Maggie's room was more than just somber. It was choking. Rhys sat on the bed next to her small body. He held her hand and looked over at her. It's funny how someone never seems small or fragile until they are still. Unable to move around or boast about ridiculous plans. Even with her short stature, her robust personality and energy made her feel so much larger.

Maggie's chest fluttered, showing her struggle with capturing those hollow breaths. Her skin lost its usual warmth and honey tone and sweat drenched her hair and the pillow she rested on. This was more than the symptoms of a bump on the head. Maggie was sick, and she wasn't getting better.

I could sense it, darkness, it was all around the room, and it was trying to infect Maggie. This was Alderic's work. His dark energy preyed on her already weak and vulnerable spirit. This was my fault. Had I not used her magic as a ciphering punch bag, she would have been strong enough to defend herself from his attack.

"How is she doing?" I placed my arm on his shoulder.

"You're back!" Rhys jumped up and pulled me into his arms. "You have got to stop scaring me like that."

"I'm sorry. It wasn't my intention." He kissed me on my forehead. "Maggie?"

"She isn't doing so well." He moved back to her side. "I don't understand it. She regained consciousness when we got back, but it didn't last. She stuffed her face with mom's gumbo, then she passed back out. When I realize it wasn't just a food coma, I tried to wake her. Nothing we did helped. Mom even tried to coax her out of it with magic. Nothing."

"What can we do?" I sat on the bed next to him and laid my hand on Maggie's leg. "There must be something."

"I'm not sure." Rhys shook his head. "Best I can think of is to hope that she comes out of it? It's only been a few hours."

"So we just sit and wait?" I couldn't accept that. "There has to be more that we can do."

"I'm not sure what that would be at this point." Rhys said.

"Right, okay." I stood, pulling my hair up into a bun. "No, I don't accept that. I won't sit here and watch her die."

"What are you doing?"

"Something. More than just sitting here." I held my hands out to her and focused. It took some doing because I was still weak from all that happened, but soon my energy flowed from my palms over to Maggie's resting body.

I kept it up for ten of the longest seconds of my life. Then Maggie choked. Her eyelids fluttered and her body seized. "What's happening?" I asked, but I already knew the answer. Maggie was losing the battle; my father was winning. Even with my energy, he would claim her and her magic for his own.

"I don't know." Rhys moved to the door, pulled it opened and yelled for help. "Mom!"

I couldn't wait for them, for anyone. She needed me to help. I jumped onto the bed, straddling her, and placed my hands on her arms. I could do more if she let me. My arms gripped her tightly, but nothing happened. "Maggie, please let me help you!" I screamed at her. "Stop being so damn stubborn!"

With all of my anger, I felt it; the heat at the palm of my hands grew and jolted her body. Her pain stopped for a moment, but it returned, the shaking of her limbs much more intense the second time around. The evil of my father's magic attacked her with more aggression than before. I would not lose her to him.

I lifted her at the shoulders to pull her into a sitting position, wrapped my arms around her, and held her tightly to my chest. "You cannot have her!" I whispered to my father. He could hear me. If his magic was there, so was he.

I took a deep breath and focused on Maggie's magic, that part of her that had slipped away, but still held on to her by the slightest thread.

If I could cipher magic into myself, I could cipher it through me. I called to her energy and felt it move in through my back and out through my chest to find itself back where it belonged, its home. With each passing moment, Maggie's spirit returned and my father's dark magic retreated.

Her tremors stopped, and her eyes opened. "Sy?" She coughed my name. "Why are you straddling me?"

I pulled her tighter into my arms, relieved that for

once, it seemed I had done something right.

"Omg, please say that you are okay!" I rubbed my fingers through her short curls like she was a child left in my care.

"Well, it looks like that power move of yours works both ways." She choked out, and when I released her from my hold had a lazy smile on her face. "I feel high!"

"Oh, I am so happy you're alright!" tears fell from my eyes. I couldn't believe I was so close to losing her.

"What's wrong?" Roxanne entered the room holding her chest, my mother and Ebon were right on her heels.

"It was Maggie. She seized, but she is okay now." Rhys reported and returned to the bedside.

"How?" Roxanne asked as she moved to examine the patient.

"Sy," Maggie smiled when I moved from the bed.

"I just, I did what felt right." I looked at Ebon, fearing that she would not approve of the method I had chosen, but she smiled at me and nodded.

That nod relieved my chest of the tight hold of anxiety. She was not just there to help us take down Alderic; she was the spiritual ancestor of the witch covens, the very coven that wanted to get rid of me. If she felt I had abused my power, she could strike me down whenever she pleased.

Because nothing was sacred, no moment sweet enough to deserve sanctuary, a forceful pounding interrupted the momentary relief we all felt. And just like that, everyone in the room stiffened. As far as we knew, no one was coming to visit. Who would dare to visit the house where the dangerous hybrid stayed? Whoever this was, was no friend.

"I'll get it." Rhys announced before leaving the room. I wanted to follow him, but needed to make sure Maggie was okay first.

"Are you sure you're okay?" Roxanne took my place by Maggie's side. "You look a little out of it."

"Yes, I feel great." Maggie pushed herself back against the headboard. "I just think whatever Sy did came with some fun side effects. Your hair has stars in it!"

"Syrinada!" Rhys reluctantly called from downstairs. The visitor was for me, but from the tense tone of his voice, he didn't think that I would want to see who it was. "There is someone here to see you."

"Why doesn't that sound like a good thing?" I muttered before leaving the room. "Who could possibly be visiting me here?"

The only people I knew in the area, besides the members of the coven who wanted me dead, were inside the house. Anyone else was unwelcomed. I froze midway down the stairs as the untimely visitor came into view. "Aunt Noreen?"

"Syrinada," she looked at me almost lovingly. She'd had so many years to perfect that false expression. Just another mask she stored in her bag of tricks. It wasn't one I would fall for again. She didn't love me, loathe was more like it.

"Noreen, what are you doing here?" My mother stood at the top of the stairs, looking down at us.

"Sister? You're alive. I thought- he said you died!" Noreen took a step forward, but Rhys blocked her from entering the house. She peeked around him at her sister. "How is this possible?"

"Well, he, as we all now know, is a liar." My mother spoke and descended the steps further to join me at the bottom step.

"Where have you been? You look..." Noreen's shock was palpable. She knew she would find me there. Probably had some plan to regain my favor, but she wasn't expecting to see her sister again.

"That is not important. Why are you here?" My mother stepped in front of me, pushing me back with her arm. "If you came to hurt my daughter any more than you already have,"

"No, I didn't, I swear." Noreen promised.

"What do you want, then?" I asked, but Noreen spoke to my mother only.

"I'm so sorry for everything that I did to you and to Syrinada. My apology cannot erase the hurt that I caused you, but that is all that I have to offer you. I thought, I thought he loved me, that he would keep me with him. He said that he and I and Sy, that the three of us, we would be a family."

"You would take that away from me so willingly. Why?" The hurt in my mother's voice was agonizing. I wanted to hold on to her. We'd lost so much time together because of the selfish acts of others.

"You could never understand. You already had everything. Everything that I could not. I could not conceive his child because it would never be as strong, as beautiful, or as powerful." Noreen choked up. "I met him before you, even though you would come to think differently. He wanted it that way.

"We shared so much together. I thought he and I would be together forever. I was ready to tell everyone about us, but he changed. He asked me for a strand of my hair so he could perform some magical test. When he did, it proved that I was... inadequate. He asked that I bring him one of yours and, like a fool, I did.

"Your genetics, that code that makes you who you are now, was what he needed. I was not enough. I didn't see it at the time, but he was testing the power in us." Noreen's eyes flooded with tears as she adjusted the thin jacket she wore.

"Where your results presented a well of strength, though still untapped, mine showed that my power was all but nonexistent. So I helped him out of foolishness, out of love. I gave him everything he asked of me, not knowing what it would do to us all." Noreen was crying; tears that even a blind person could tell were not for show. Alderic had broken her heart, and it was breaking all over again right in front of us.

"You wanted love, which is no excuse for betraying your family! You had love! I loved you!" My mother fumed. She gripped my hand, and I acted as her anchor. "We all loved you, Noreen! You were my everything long before that warlock walked into our lives! I trusted you with my heart. With my daughter!"

"It's not an excuse; it's the truth of what happened. I love him and I would give him anything he asked of me. Even my own life."

"What?" My mother stepped forward, a frown of disgust painted her face. "You still feel this way? How could you say that after everything that happened?"

"It's the truth." New tears fell from her eyes, her expression no longer a mournful reflection of a past tragedy. This was something different. It felt almost like an omen, like something bad was about to happen. "I know what you want me to say. If I were stronger, I would turn my back on him, but I can't. He is in me. Woven into the very fibers of my being. I love him."

"Why are you here?" I couldn't listen to it anymore. She pandered over my deadbeat father as if he was some gift from above. How could anyone be so blinded by affection?

"I am here, with a message from your father." she turned to me. "Join him, or suffer the same fate."

"The same fate?" I looked up the stairs to where Maggie was. She was safe. I could still feel it. So what was Noreen talking about? "The same fate as who?"

"As me." Tears fell from her eyes, first clear, then crimson.

Noreen stumbled as she coughed and blood spilled from her lips. I watched with mixed emotions. It was horrifying, yes, and yet I was okay. I didn't want her to hurt, or to die, but after everything she'd done, I found it difficult to feel any remorse.

"Sister, no!" My mother ran to her Noreen, pushed past Rhys, and caught my falling aunt in her arms just before she hit the floor. "Please. No, don't die!" She cradled her head in her lap and sobbed. "I just returned. We lost so much time, I can't lose you." Blood quickly stained her skin and the white gown she wore as her little sister's life slipped away.

I wanted to help. If I could have, I would have. If only so that my mother wouldn't suffer, but there was nothing left of Noreen. She told the truth. Alderic's evil flooded her entire being. There was nothing left of Noreen, of the woman she used to be. When I looked at her aura, all I saw was his.

She was but a puppet, and her master hid behind the veils of his dark magic. My mother clutched her sister as tightly as she could, as if the force alone would stop the life from draining from her limbs. There was nothing we could do.

"I love you." Noreen reached up to touch her older sister's face before her eyes slid shut for the last time.

CHAPTER
14

*W*e *mourned.*

The entire house and all of its guests fell under the soul-crushing burden of sorrow. My mother's emotion infiltrated us all. It even filled the room where Roxanne worked her magic to calm restless spirits with a choking somber.

Rhys removed Noreen's body from the foyer after my mother finally let her go. Her body had to be prepared for the ceremony to send her back to the seas. I never thought of what a siren funeral would look like. If I had my choice, I'd never have to experience one.

Time was not on our side, and the ceremony had to be done quickly. To allow too much time to pass would be to allow for vulnerability that could be used against us. This was something my calculating father would count on.

Roxanne cleaned and dressed the body with the guidance of my mother, who tended to her sister as if she were burying her own child. Each time she sobbed, the atmosphere became that much more depressing. This was the strength my father sought. This was the power he wanted. Even without trying, even without her stone, my mother was impressively influential.

"Do you feel that?" Sitting at the desk in my room and preparing myself for what was to come, I asked Rhys, who hadn't left my side since they excused him from his duties as my mother's aid.

"Yes, your mother, she is amazing." Every single breath she took, we felt.

"Rhys," My mind was heavy with worry, with concern for all the changes that were happening.

"What's wrong?" he asked, then corrected himself. "I'm sorry, that was insensitive, given the circumstances."

"No, it's not that. This new ability of mine, which allows me to pull in power…" how could I express what I felt without causing him to look at me differently? How could I avoid having him worry about my sanity?

"Syrinada," he knew exactly what I was getting at.

"I hate that I want to do it. I hate that it feels so

enticing, and I know it is wrong." I stared at my hands because I needed to focus on something other than his eyes, which I was sure held disappointment at my inability to control myself. "She's my mother. This is what he wanted, isn't it? He wanted me to feel what lives inside of her. He wants me to take her power into me."

"You won't do that." He reassured me. "You are stronger than what he wants from you."

"How can you continue to be so sure of me when no one else is even remotely capable?" I dropped my shoulders, releasing some of the tension there. "Hell, I'm not even so sure anymore."

"I am sure of you because I have watched you do amazing things. You put others above yourself, you breathe life into things that have none, you are selfless, and that is what characterizes you. Your actions dictate who you are, not your father's wishes." Rhys knelt before me, forcing me to look at him and not my intertwined fingers.

"When I look at you, I don't see him. I see her, your mother. That same love, that same desire and willingness to nurture those around you and protect those you care for. That is your mother in you, not your father."

The tears in my eyes contradicted the smile on my face as I gazed at him. The last remnants of the sun peered through the window to touch his face. Inside of me, there was movement, a powerful surge, that shifted my vision, and my love lit up.

He stood in front of me, pulling me to my feet, and a halo of light I knew only I could see it appeared around him. I wished like hell that I could tell my mother, ask her what it meant, but that would have to wait. What I knew was what I felt for Rhys was real, and it was undeniable.

~*~

We moved through the night by magical transport, provided by the combined efforts of Rhys, Roxanne, and Ebon. Our group had grown, and it took more power to make the move. We appeared under the night sky back at the mouth of the sea.

Resting on a bed of woven weeds and flowers, one that shouldn't have been able to hold the weight of a leaf, let alone an entire person, we set Noreen out onto the water. We lit our candles and watched as her tail emerged for the last time as she floated away.

No one spoke, and the light from the candles we held flickered. The wind picked up just enough to cause soft ripples along the surface of the still seas. My mother moved forward until she was waist deep in the water. The long dress she wore, white and gold with lace, moved around her body along with the tides. She dropped her head back to bathe in the moon's light.

We all watched her and waited. My heart smiled as she sang a song I once thought I'd never be able to hear. Her siren song. This was different, though, a variation of what I'd expected. It wasn't meant to lure any man. This was a song of testimony, of love, and of forgiveness. As her octave raised, the waters opened up and swallowed the body of her sister.

Rhys took my candle as I joined her in the water. My dress, long and red, twisted in the water with the fabric of her dress. She had been through so much; she should never have to be alone in anything so tough. Hand in hand, I caught her melody and allowed our voices to blend. The sea danced a calm ballet, and the sky lit up as if the stars wanted to join in.

"Thank you, Syrinada." My mother turned to me and kissed my cheek.

"I'm so sorry. I wish there was more that I could do." In the water, I wrapped my arms around my mother and laid my head on her shoulder. The pain I felt was not for my aunt, it was for my mother. It was for her loss, her pain.

"You helped me send her home, calling to the seas and the heavens. You have brought me peace yet again." She kissed my forehead and turned away from the open water.

With my arm around her waist, and her own wrapped around my shoulder, we walked back to the group, who stared at us in awe. Rhys smiled as if it were punctuation on our earlier conversation. He was right; I was my mother's child.

The house felt lighter when we returned, yet everyone remained silent as we moved through the halls. Roxanne prepared a feast that we all devoured in hushed enjoyment. Good rest was what we needed, with a full belly, that wouldn't be hard to accomplish.

They gave my mother Rhys' room, and he was eager to accommodate her needs and moved to the couch downstairs. I wanted to suggest that he bunk with me, but couldn't bring myself to say the words with both his and my mother's eyes on me. What message would that send? What conversation would it start? Neither topic was one that I felt like facing at the moment.

As everyone settled in for what remained of the night, my mind kicked into high gear. Lying across the bed, still completely dressed with the water from my wet clothing seeping through the sheets into the mattress, the noise inside of my head would not silence. How much more could go wrong? How long would my father lurk in the shadows before enacting whatever he had planned next?

Would I be strong enough to defend us all against him? At least I wasn't alone. I had friends and family and for the first time, that word didn't scare me. Family. It didn't depress the hell out of me. Well, it did, but for an entirely different reason. Family. It used to hurt because

I had none, and now it caused a stinging sensation in the pit of my stomach because there was nothing more important to me. Family. It had to be protected, it had to be kept safe.

"Syrinada," Rhys whispered as he gently slid the door open and stepped inside of my room. I looked at him and smiled, glad that he risked total maternal annihilation to come to me.

"You." My lips curved as he walked across the room to join me.

"I couldn't stay away. I felt drawn to you." He admitted. "You shouldn't be alone tonight."

"Is that good or bad?" I moved over to allow room for him to fit next to me.

"Oh, it's good." He slid into the bed, moving me to my side and scooping my body so that my back pressed against his chest. "You're soaking wet."

"The water from the sea feels so good against my skin; I wasn't ready to remove it." I smiled. "Does it bother you?"

"It's a little cold." He chuckled. "What about now? Would it be okay to remove it now?"

"Yeah, I think that would be okay." He moved to his knees, and I returned to my position on my back.

Slowly, he pulled the dress down my shoulders, across my hips and revealed the little black lingerie beneath. He left me there for a moment as he disappeared into the adjoined bathroom. When he returned, he held a dark towel, which he lay beneath my legs to cover the wet spot on the mattress left behind from the dress.

From a bin beneath the bed, he pulled out an additional sheet and blanket. Rhys covered me in them and climbed into bed. He only covered himself with the blanket; he left the sheet between us, a barrier between our flesh. I smiled because it made me happy to know how considerate and kindhearted he was, and I smirked because there was a part of me that wished that he wasn't such a gentleman.

"Are you comfortable?" His breath was a warm brush at the back of my neck.

"Yes, I am." I grabbed his arm and pulled it tighter around me and scooted as close as I could to his body.

He kissed me goodnight after we lay in each other's arms. I needed that. His warmth, his strength. Things had changed so severely in such a short time. It had barely been six months since a drug addict in a beat-up car flipped my life upside down. I wouldn't have believed it then that this was where I'd be, after all the horror, that there'd be peace and comfort. In the morning, I would thank him for bringing that back into my life.

CHAPTER
15

Forceful impact rudely erased a dream of the deep blue of the sea. I flowed through the waters, flexing my tail to push me into the depths and then shooting upward to break through the surface like a free-living dolphin. Just as I dove again to gain momentum, that feeling of total and complete comfort, of stability, and freedom, shattered as the bedroom walls shook.

I awoke from my dream to what felt like an earthquake. Rhys tightened his hold on me as the walls of the house shook and the figurines on the nightstand fell and shattered against the floor.

"What the hell is that?" I screamed. Did New Orleans have earthquakes? My groggy mind couldn't remember. Damn it! I wanted to be back in the sea!

"I don't know! Hold on." The shaking lasted a little while longer before the floors steadied and we could get out of bed. Along with everyone else, we ran down the stairs and out the front door to what felt safer. Hell, if the house was about to collapse, we didn't want to be inside of it!

"Is everyone okay? Did everyone make it out?" Roxanne frantically counted heads and held on to my mother's hand.

"We're all okay, we're here." Maggie spoke and tried to calm Roxanne, who looked like she would faint.

"I warned you!" We turned to the voice that rang out in the darkness behind us.

Standing, in black cloaks, like a scene from every horror movie I'd ever seen, were the witches of New Orleans. Front and center was Marlo, the old witch that lead the coven. She was the only one to drop her hood. The others stood in silence, awaiting her command.

Even with their faces covered by their hoods, I recognized the two directly at her sides. They were the ones who manhandled me at her command when Maggie took me to be judged. Each of the witches that accompanied her chanted a familiar spell. It was a spell that called for strength. It transferred that collected strength to one person. Marlo. Great, the wicked witch of the bayou.

"I did nothing wrong!" I shouted at the old lady.

I knew she intended her declaration for me. No one else in the house had any dealings with her. She'd been waiting for anything to use against me. Anything to give her the right to take me out.

"You think we weren't watching? Did you think we would really let you run around, the abomination that you are, without keeping tabs on you? We knew Margaret would betray us. She is weak and too fascinated by you." She pointed at the girl who bristled at her words. "Just as I thought she would, she turned her back on our cause."

"I did no such thing!" Maggie marched forward, prepared to defend herself. "If you want to go off on some lynching job, you do that on your own time! Sy met with the spirits, and they called off your little hunt! Despite what you seem to think, I do not answer to you, Marlo!"

"Silence child!" Maggie fell to her knees under the weight of the power Marlo threw at her.

Maggie was strong, but after all that she'd been through, her body and mind were weak. There still hadn't been time for her to recover. I flinched at her pain, but held my ground. I would not retaliate. Marlo was smart. If I did anything, it would give her exactly what she wanted.

"Which of my actions is it you claim to be deserving of all of this?" I stepped forward. "What could you have possibly seen that you would risk the lives of these people just to get to me?"

"You think stealing the magic of others is okay? Even if it is your god awful father, it is still against our ways!" Marlo seethed. "Then to filter that evil into Margaret, to taint her soul in such a way. I can smell the filth on her! You are a monster and we must deal with you appropriately!"

The others who joined her chanted louder. As they increased their efforts, Roxanne and Rhys moved to stand by my side. They grabbed hands and began a low chant of their own. Marlo wanted a war, and she brought it to our front door.

"You have no right to be here! You are the one hurting her right now, not me!" I balled my fist at my side. It was one thing to be accused of doing something wrong, but to say that I intentionally hurt Maggie or anyone else that I loved was where I drew the line.

"Oh, I have every reason to be here. Look at yourself. Right now, anger fills your heart and darkens your soul." She smiled. "You think you can take me, child? Do it!"

"Leave here. Leave us alone and do not return." I warned her. We both knew what I was capable of and she was only goading me.

"Or what?" Marlo tilted her head and Maggie

moaned as the bitch witch increased the power she used on her.

"I will not fight you! I know that is what you want. You know you have no reason to be here. No case against me or this sad display of power wouldn't be necessary. Admit it, if you had any right, if the ancestors knew you were here, there would be no need for discussion. I would already be dead!"

"Holding back now won't save you, girl! We already know what you are capable of, and what you can and will do if we allow you to roam free!"

"Leave her alone!" Maggie screamed and tried to fight free, but she was nowhere near strong enough.

"You will be quiet! Traitor, you turned your back on your own kind." With her power, she lifted Maggie from the ground and pulled her over to her. Maggie's feet hung in the air before her. Her face turned red, and she struggled to breathe. "Give me one good reason I shouldn't end you right along with the abomination you betrayed your people for!"

Eyes locked on me, Marlo pulled her hand back and slapped Maggie hard enough for blood to spill from her lips.

"Lay another hand on her and I will give you every reason you came looking for." I spoke.

"Oh, is that so?" She pulled back and with every bit of her strength, slammed her palm into Maggie's face. The whimper of her lips was enough to make me snap.

"Syrinada, don't do it." Rhys laid a hand on my shoulder. "This isn't worth it. You can't give her what she wants."

"I can't let her keep hurting my friend." I stepped away from him and focused on Marlo.

She smiled because she knew that she'd gotten exactly what she came for. She was ready for a fight. Rhys and Roxanne increased the speed of their chant. Even if they didn't agree with my decision to fight, they would continue to protect me.

"You shouldn't have come here!" The small figure of a girl long deceased appeared in the middle of the field.

When I saw her, I felt the rush of calm flow over me and the anger that was consuming me dissipated. Ebon had hidden herself, allowed the scene to play out as it would naturally. This was a test, but this time I wasn't the one being tested.

"Ebon? I..." Marlo panicked and her eyes bulged as they darted between our faces, as if she was trying to see if her eyes were the only ones that captured the spirit. Her witch crew stopped chanting and replaced their mantras with prayers of forgiveness. "She betrayed us!

She broke the rules!"

"She broke no rules. And even if that were true, since when is it your position to cast such judgments?" The power that was in Ebon's voice brought a deathly sharpness to the air.

Hers was the blended tone of many. I recognized the voices of the others. The deep tone of the ghost whose name I dare not ask to know, and the cool air of Amelia, the spirit who appeared to me with dark skin, a smooth bald head, and large golden hoops in her ears. There were others I didn't recognize as well; ones who sounded so powerful, it scared me.

"I did what the ancestors tasked me to do. It is my job to police these demons and these hybrids." Marlo defended her actions. "I promised to protect our people."

"What you seem to forget is that this girl, this abomination, as I have so often heard you refer to her, is a part of our people. She is of our blood. It is you who has strayed, not her or Margaret. Look at what you've done to this girl." She kneeled down to touch Maggie's cheek. "You are no longer working in the best interest of our people. For that reason, your services are no longer required." She spoke her judgment without returning her gaze to Marlo.

"What?" The old woman stomped her feet like a

child having a tantrum. "No! This isn't right! You can't
_"

"You will go home, and you will think of your actions. And you will pray the ancestors have mercy on your soul."

"I will not. I will not allow them to ruin what we have here!" She turned towards me with the anger of a thousand jaded witches and held her hand out to me.

I could feel it, the magic she stirred inside, the power she planned to use against me. The darkness that dwelled inside of her. For someone who spent so much time trying to cleanse the world of evil, she sure had a lot living inside her own twisted heart. I flinched as she yelled out her declaration, her desire to end my life.

"It's time for you to die, girl!"

CHAPTER
16

Instead of feeling pain of my own, I witnessed hers. Her body froze, limbs rigid, and eyes widened in fear. She tried to speak, but only frightened mumbles were audible. Ebon stood from her place, where she knelt beside Maggie and walked towards the covens' newly disgraced leader.

As she neared her, Ebon's small body lifted from the ground until the two were at eye level. Floating in front of Marlo, she looked more like the ghost that she was. Her body became translucent and her skin glowed with the light of the afterlife. With the tip of her finger, she pushed the Marlo's greyed head back, and pressed the palm of her left hand against the frightened witch's open chest.

"You've turned your back on the ways of our people and used your power for deeds of evil and selfish means. You, Marlo, are no longer worthy of all that flows through you. I return your power to its rightful place with the ancestors." Ebon's voice booms around us, shaking the ground beneath our feet as she continued. "Marlo, you are no longer with us, no longer of us. I condemn you and revoke your right to exist with our kind."

By defying the direct orders of the ancestors, Marlo had lost her right to lead the coven. Those who followed her wouldn't be punished, at least not as severely. For Marlo, there would be no second chance, no hope of undoing all the evil she'd done. For her defiance, Ebon stripped her of her powers completely.

"You will leave here and you will not return. If you decide to disregard our wishes, we will not give you the opportunity to walk away a second time." Ebon dropped her hands to her side and returned to the ground where she stood, shoulders straight, and head held high, as she watched Marlo whimper and retreat.

No one followed the dishonored witch, not a single one of the witches who so easily aided her. There was no loyalty to the disgraced. They stood in wait for their own judgment to be cast.

"Now. Someone will have to take her place. The coven cannot go on without a leader." Ebon turned from the praying witches, completely unconcerned with their fears, no matter how warranted. Kneeling beside Maggie, Roxanne looked up at Ebon, who returned to her corporeal form and watched her closely. "You."

"Me?" she questioned nervously. "I'm not exactly a fan favorite around these parts."

"This is exactly why they need you to lead. Our people have lost their way and you are the one person who will put them back on the right path."

"I," Roxanne stood and looked at Rhys, who smiled with pride.

"The decision is made. We will perform the ritual tomorrow night beneath the high moon." Ebon gave Roxanne no other choice; this apparently wasn't a topic that would be up for debate. That wasn't at all surprising.

The magical realm often thrusted significant life changes upon people. There were no true choices. You did what you had to do. Roxanne nodded and looked at the group of witches, who stared at her in anticipation. I wished I could see Roxanne induction as the coven's new leader, but it was a closed practice.

The ceremony would happen with the ancestral spirits. Usually the previous leader would pass on the torch, but being that she was no longer with her power, Marlo wouldn't receive an invitation either. There would be a public celebration at a later date where they would officially announce her new role and she would take her position as the coven's new leader.

~*~

"Sy, is it okay if I come in?" Maggie spoke from the

other side of my bedroom door. After the witches left Roxanne's home, we all returned to our respective areas to survey the damage Marlo had done. Fortunately, it wasn't nearly as bad as it felt. She only meant the controlled tremors to flush us all out of the house, which they did.

"Yes, of course, come in." When she stepped through the door and closed it behind her, I rushed over to her so that I could inspect her. Not only had my father had nearly taken away from us her but also now, she was standing up to her own people. How much could one girl go through before she cracked? "Are you okay?"

"Yes, I'm fine. Stop worrying about me; it's not good for you." She stepped away from my fluttering hands and sat on the foot of the bed. "I just need to talk to you."

"It's hard for me not to worry about you, considering everything that is going on. You've been through so much and, to be honest, there is some guilt accompanying that worry."

"You don't have to feel guilty about anything. I make my own decisions, my own choices." Maggie pointed to her chest. "Everything that happens to me happens because I choose for it to happen."

"About that." There was so much I didn't know about her, so much that was still a mystery to me. Watching her suffer at the hands of Marlo made me realize that I'd never taken the time to get to know her.

"Why did you decide to go against the coven? I mean, it feels like there is something more there, something you aren't telling us."

"I guess I should have expected this question to come up at some point." She smiled and looked at the ceiling. "I've been told since I was a little girl that I was different, that I did things in a way that wasn't normal. From the time that I could walk, my grandmother impressed upon me to accept my fate, to love my life for every moment and to never compromise myself for the will of anyone else.

"Marlo changed the coven. I watched it happen, and it didn't take centuries. It only took a few years. She took over and shifted things to match her cold and paranoid mindset. We were so close at one time. She was my best friend, but my mother changed. Something dark touched her heart and it just never let go."

"Marlo is your mother?" My mouth fell open, and I quickly shut it. Maggie looked nothing like her mother.

"Yes, she is." She shrugged, then leaned over to look out the window as if her mother would be outside.

"How could you not tell me? I'm so sorry, Maggie." I sat down beside her and pulled her into my arms. Here she was, helping me save my mother while protecting me from hers. She was so strong, yet I couldn't help but fear what was coming for her.

"It's okay, trust me. I've dealt with the truth of who

I am and where I come from. I have accepted that she was once the greatest part of my life. People change, things change. She taught me to stay true to myself, even if that meant turning my back on her."

"What about your grandmother? Where is she?"

"She's long gone. I think losing her is what made my mother snap. There was never any proof, but they said a siren did it. That one of your kind killed her. It never made sense to me. My grandmother was no high priestess, but she wasn't weak. She was strong and could defend her own. Nothing about it ever felt right. I tried to get my mother to see it, to look deeper and find the person really responsible for her death. She refused to. That was when she first called me a traitor. That is when she sent me away. On the hunt to find more 'abominations'."

"I don't know what to say. I just wish I could make this all better for you." Could it have been possible that a siren was responsible for the death of Maggie's grandmother? If it were true, it would make perfect sense for Marlo to have such hatred for my kind and me.

"There's something I need you to do, something I know that you have been avoiding." A topic change seemed appropriate, but something told me I would miss the discussion about the misguided Marlo. "Know that I wouldn't ask this of you if I didn't think that it was absolutely necessary."

"Okay," I hesitated. "What is it?"

174

"You need to reach out to Malachi and Demetrius. You need to ask them to come here, to help us." She grabbed my hand and looked me in the eye.

There was fear there that hadn't been before. I knew it was impossible for her to have gone through so much and suffer no adverse effect. I witnessed that aftermath play out in the pupils of her eyes. She was terrified, and she had every right to be. Her own mother had just tried to kill her, and my damaged daddy was coming for us. Talk about parental issues.

"I can't do that." I shook my head no. They deserved to be free of me. It was a promise I made to myself. Leave them to themselves and let them be happy without interference.

"You can, and you have to." She stepped to me and forced me to look at her. "It sucks, yeah, but you know you need to do this. I know you want to believe that we got this on our own, but we cannot do this without their help. All sides must come together to defeat your father."

"What makes you think they will want to help me?" After everything that I had done, after all the heartache and pain that I had caused the brothers, they would have to be out of their minds to still want to do anything that would benefit me.

"The better question is, do you really believe that they won't?" She grabbed my hand and pulled me back to the bed to where we sat in silence.

I contemplated what she asked me. I knew she was right. Regardless of what went down between us, Malachi and Demetrius would come if I were to call. It wouldn't be just because I was a siren. It would be because they truly wanted to be there for me and to help me out. That's what really worried me. Not that they wouldn't come, but that they would. They would come to save me and I would hurt them all over again.

CHAPTER
17

"**They aren't coming. Just let it go.**" I addressed
Maggie, who asked me about the brothers for
the hundredth. "It's been a week since I called to them."

I had hidden my disappointment from Rhys, but
she could tell that something was bothering me. It
was much easier to confess my worries to her. We had
become so close in such a short time. Besides, telling her
wouldn't add any extra stress to my life. It wasn't like
there was any risk of her getting upset or jealous over
my concerns about the Denali brothers.

"Do you think something broke the bond
between you?" She tried to offer another reason for
their unresponsiveness. "Maybe they don't know you
reached out to them."

"No, I can definitely still feel Demetrius. He is just
not answering my call." It felt terrible, being able to feel

someone who wanted nothing to do with me.

For a time, I could block out my connection to him, but since calling him, I'd been unable to get away from the feeling of his life being tied to my own. What made it worse was the intense rush of his happiness just moments before I called to him. When I opened that mental door again, his joy came rushing through the connection. Wherever he was and whoever he was with, he was at peace. He was loved, and it was an amazing thing.

That happiness, however, was quickly replaced with feelings of resentment and sorrow. He wanted nothing to do with me. Who could blame him after all that I had put him and his brother through? I felt for Malachi, but there was no sign of his presence, and I could tell that he was nowhere near Demetrius, either.

"That is impossible, right? I mean, doesn't that go against the laws of nature with you sirens?" Maggie put her hand on my shoulder, not sure what else to say or do. There honestly wasn't anything else I could ask of her, but to lend me her ear.

"No, not really. Just because she calls doesn't mean that he has to answer." We both looked up at my mother, who stood in the open doorway.

With the wind that flowed through my bedroom window lifting her hair, it was hard not to stare at her. She was beautiful, though she looked barely a few years older than I did. Each time I saw her, I had the urge to get up and hug her, but I sat still and listened to what she had to say. She'd heard our entire conversation because we hadn't thought to close the door behind us. We weren't concerned about being overheard by Rhys, who was out of the house running errands for his mother.

"Just most often they when one calls, her mate answers. Though we wish it were true, they do can ignore us." She continued. "I suppose that's why we have such an intense fascination with the human males. They're weaker and have no choice but to do as we command."

"I guess we're on our own then. I can't force them to come and clearly, they don't want to. This was a bad idea." I stood from my bed and wiped away tears that threatened to reveal just how sad their absence made me.

I missed them both, especially Malachi. Besides Tasha, he'd been my best friend. Too bad my complicated existence ruined everything. I lost someone who meant the world to me, and it was my own damn fault.

"I need to take a walk. Some fresh air may help clear my mind." I headed for the door.

"Don't worry, Sy, I will still look for others to help us. There are a few favors I can call in." Maggie pulled me back into a hug before I could get away.

I wrapped my arms around her in a tight hug. Despite everything, she always tried to keep a positive perspective, even when the chips were so devastatingly stacked against us.

"Thanks, Maggie." I tightened my arms around her. "You know how much I appreciate having you here, right?"

"Yeah, I know. I'm the peanut butter to your jelly." She laughed, and I couldn't help but join her. The girl was so corny sometimes.

"Would you like me to join you?" My mother asked as I scooted past her to get through the doorway.

"No, I'll be okay. Some alone time may actually be just what I need." Her hand felt wonderful, a caress of love as she touched my face, nodded her understanding, and let me walk away.

Outside, it was quiet, but the silence had become a necessity. My mind made enough noise on its own without the additional chatter produced by those who surrounded me. That house seemed so loud, even when no one spoke. It was so full of their expectations and anticipation. Everyone knew I had called to my former protectors and asked that they come to aid us. Everyone knew both brothers had denied my call.

My stroll took me into the forested lands behind Roxanne's house. The covering of trees that led to the bayous. There was no aim for my walk. This was pure mindless action. Keep walking as longs as it meant I could be free of the chaos. If only for just a moment.

"You're looking good. Stronger." The low voice spoke from behind me, and I froze.

Have you ever wanted something so badly that it hurt you? It hurt not to have it and it hurt even more to think for a second that there could actually be a chance that you could get it. If that moment of elation turned out to be just a trick your mind was playing on you, wishful thinking, or some sick cosmic joke, it would crush you entirely.

My feet stopped moving, frozen; I tried my best to steady my heart before turning toward the voice. It had to be him; this couldn't be a game someone was playing on me. That voice, that deep, soulful tone which still held evidence of the hurt I had caused him, it just had to be him.

"Malachi." I whispered before turning, as if saying his name would cause him to materialize. Maybe it worked, maybe it didn't, but when I turned, my heart soared. "You're here."

He was there, tall, bald, and brooding. He looked good, just upset, and angry with me. The urge to approach him was powerful, but my legs wouldn't move. I had no right. It wasn't my place. I shouldn't have even called him. He deserved peace; he deserved to be free of me.

"Did you really think I wouldn't show up for you?" He walked closer to me and I focused on the sound of the ground crunching beneath his feet to avoid the anger in his eyes. He'd never hurt me, not the Malachi I knew, but was this that same caring soul, or someone else entirely? "I just wanted to give you and my brother time to get reacquainted before I popped up. I figured you would have called him too."

"You're not with Demetrius?" I frowned, then relaxed, because I knew they weren't together. I felt their distance in the connection with Demetrius and how hurt he was that their relationship suffered.

"No, my brother and I parted ways after you left. You're telling me he isn't here?" He looked back in the house's direction. Demetrius wasn't there; he hadn't come.

"I assumed he would be with you." I dropped my head and checked my tone. It couldn't look like I was too disappointed about his brother not being there.

"We didn't exactly work things out as one might have hoped. You were gone. He blamed me, and I blamed him." He looked at me and shrugged as if the rift in their relationship didn't deeply bother him, but I could see in his eyes that it did.

Demetrius was the only family he had. As much

as family meant to Malachi, I knew that this wasn't something he could easily get over.

"I'm so sorry; I never meant to come between you two." What else was there to say? I still kept my distance. Just because he was here didn't mean he wanted to be close to me.

"We put you there," he shrugged and moved to lean against a tree. "That was so messed up. I've thought about it a lot. We asked you to choose between us when your life was already in turmoil. We were supposed to be protecting you, Sy. It was unfair for us to put you in that position."

"How have you been?" The wind kicked up, and I pulled my hair back to keep it from blocking my vision of him.

"Drunk, mostly." The deep chuckle raised small ridges at the corner of his mouth. When he dropped his head back to stare at the sky, I noticed the missing medallion he usually wore around his neck.

"Where is your medallion?" They had charmed the piece with magic to keep the darker side of my protector at bay.

Malachi was a merman, but he was something else as well, another hybrid like me. Only, his other half wasn't a witch, it was a demon. Without that charm, Malachi would shift into his demonic self. How was he keeping the shift at bay?

"In a safe place. I've been working on containing the beast on my own. From the look on your face, I guess I am not doing such a great job at that."

"I'm just glad you're here, and that you are alright, mostly." It explained the way he looked and the energetic change I felt being near him.

Even though he stood in a relaxed stance, his jaw was tight, which left his expression strained. Just beneath the surface was a demon waiting to be unleashed and there was no doubt in my mind that if he let it free, that demon would attempt to rip my head off. Malachi cared about me deeply, but I could never be so sure about that other side of him.

"Yeah, well, when the siren calls, I answer." He smirked and turned his head from me to look towards the house again. What exactly was he expecting to find there?

"Malachi, I-"

"Sy, seriously, don't keep apologizing to me for what happened. It won't change anything and it won't allow us to move on. You and I both need to move forward with our lives. That has to happen now. What's done is done. Neither of us will heal if you're constantly beating yourself up about the past and then saying you're sorry for it." He sighed, "Trust me, that is not something that I want."

"You're right, we need to move on. I'll make no promises, but I'll cut down on all the apologizing." Already I struggled not to regurgitate another apology. I felt like I should offer myself up for his sacrifice, whatever it took to make things good between us again.

"Good, so tell me, where do I lay my head? I know it's still early, but Bourbon Street called to me." He chuckled and the rumble of the demon within him was there, adding a dark tremble to his tone.

He pushed away from the tree and pressed his side against mine. When he tossed his arm around my shoulder, it was hard not to flinch. My fear wasn't because of him; it was of that part of him I never fully understood.

"Right this way." I smiled and turned back toward Roxanne's house. Space was limited, but there would always be room for him. I hoped that there was a hidden cot or air mattress somewhere that he could claim.

"Now, you've gone and picked a battle with your dad. Why?" He asked, as he leaned on me.

"Trust me; it wasn't by choice at all." I struggled to walk as Malachi let more of his weight fall on my shoulders.

My father was definitely the instigator in this little

family war. He wanted a puppet, a slave to do his bidding, and I refused to be that.

"Where do we stand?" As we got closer to the house, he straightened a bit, lessening the load on my shoulders.

"Currently, we are at a standstill. He is threatening to attack, but hasn't. Mom is-"

"Mom?"

"Yes, my mother, she is still alive, after all these years. He kept her frozen in time; she barely looks a few years older than I do. I know this seems crazy, but long story short, others saw the evil in my father a long time ago." I stopped and pushed away from his weight.

"Oh, maybe you aren't that strong." he laughed.

"Whatever, anyway." I huffed before continuing. "There was a spell. Roxanne, Rhys' mother, tied my parent's lives together energetically. If one dies, so will the other. Obviously, he wouldn't allow this to happen. While I was at his home, I saw her there. I thought it was just some weird memorial, but later found out the truth. We saved her; I saved her. He isn't too pleased with me right now."

"How did you go up against him and make it out?" The question that I dreaded him asking was right there. Now I would have to go into details about my life, my new questionable talents, and myself. Now I would have to risk Malachi turning against me.

"With a lot of help and a few new gifts." I fluttered my fingers in the air, hoping to brush past the comment.

"New gifts?" There was that tone, the one that belonged to a school instructor or a guidance counselor. He was concerned, and he didn't even know that there was anything to be bothered about yet.

"Yes, I've unlocked a couple of specialty moves since I got my stone." Now wasn't the time to explain about the siphoning of power. That was too delicate a topic and, to be honest, I wasn't sure how he would take it. Malachi had always been so tough on me when it came to my magic.

"Cool, developing a new arsenal, works in our favor." Color me shocked. That was not the response I'd expected at all. Maybe there were more than just superficial changes happening to Malachi.

"Yeah, I thought so." I hesitated; maybe he was luring me into a trap. Once I got too comfortable, he would pounce and berate me with whatever punishment he saw fit.

"What else do we know?" We stood just a few yards away from the house now. Malachi stopped walking and hesitated. Was he not okay with being there? What was holding him back? Instead of inappropriately intruding on his private thoughts, I continued our conversation.

"Aunt Noreen was his puppet. She was in love with him. She betrayed my mother for that love. He didn't care about her. I doubt he was ever capable of it, not when he was already so blinded by his own evil. He fed her the false promise of love and she gave her life for that love."

"What do you mean, she gave her life?"

"She is dead. He killed her, right in front of us all, some sort of sick message. We sent her body back to the sea last week. The water, it just opened up and took her away. It was magical, and sad." I sighed, recalling the night again. "My mother, she is just so amazing. She loved Noreen despite the horrible things she did. She forgave her sister. I don't think I could be capable of the same."

"I think we both know that you are capable of a lot more than you think."

"Malachi, you've joined us." Rhys' voice called from ahead. Just as I expected, he was on his way to come find me.

"Well, a battle with the big, bad warlock daddy. How could I think to miss it?" Malachi actually seemed to be playing friendly this time around.

The last time the two met, he was very immature in his response to Rhys, who was only there to help. The coven had attacked the underwater city of Xylon, home to my siren family, not that they saw me as family. Rhys helped us to protect the city and fend off the witches.

"We're glad you're here. We can use all the help we can get." Rhys extended his hand to Malachi after he'd crossed the small distance between us.

"I'm sure. I'm at your service; just tell me where to aim." I breathed a small sigh of relief when Malachi accepted his hand and shook it.

"Look, I-" Rhys started, but my bald protector cut him off.

"Hey, you better not start going down that apology trail. I just had this conversation with the little lady here. I'm fine; it's all in the past." Malachi did that same deep chuckle and slapped Rhys on the shoulder.

"Actually, I was just going to say thank you for taking care of Syrinada all of those years. I didn't get the chance to express my gratitude for that."

"Well, you're welcome. Now, how about you take a moment to express that appreciation with a shot of whiskey?" The two laughed and walked off towards the house.

"I think you've had enough." I called out from behind them.

Malachi looked over his shoulder at me and smiled.

"Yes, ma'am! Nap, and then coffee it is for me."

"Coffee with a shot of…" Rhys trailed off, and Malachi burst out in laughter.

"Ah, he catches on quickly this one!" Malachi called out between laughs.

Okay, maybe having the two of them as pals wouldn't be such a great thing if they only worked to be negative influences on each other. I lingered on the front steps. Rhys would get Malachi squared away, and there was nothing for me to do. Besides, the hens would attack the moment he passed through the doors to the house.

Maggie would go in with her interrogation, Roxanne would start cooking up whatever food was left in the kitchen, and my mother; well, I wasn't sure what she would do. Considering that he would be the only genuine connection she had to her home. If nothing else, she would have some questions for him about their history and the changes that happened since she left.

CHAPTER 18

The night was calm. Malachi and Rhys hung out in the living room together. I thought Rhys would join me in my room, but he never did. I clearly wasn't the only one with a guilty conscience. In hindsight, it really would have been like rubbing the situation in Malachi's face.

When I turned in for the night, the two were having drinks, laughing, and telling each other a long list of insane stories. I hoped like hell that none of those tall tales included me. How terrible would it be if they spent the night sharing notes about what it was like to be with me?

Sleep was a no-go. Every time I closed my eyes, I saw either my father or Demetrius. Neither of which were actually there. My father would attack, he would start killing everyone I loved, and though Demetrius was there, he wouldn't help. Instead, he would turn his back on me and disappear.

Both were nightmares. Both left me feeling empty and confused about what my next move should be. Instead of sleeping, I found a book hidden in the nightstand's drawer under a few family photos. Rhys was adorable as a baby and gangly as a kid. I would have to make fun of his lopsided afro at a later time.

The book was black with gold dusting; the design on the cover was an intricate web of lettering. I couldn't figure out what it was supposed to read. When I tried to open it, it refused. No matter the force I put behind the effort, the damn thing wouldn't give.

It had no lock, no mechanism to bind it. There had to be some magical layer to it, something that wouldn't allow the contents to be viewed. Instead of reading the pages, I focused on the mixed-up lettering on the cover. I stared at the design for hours until the sun returned to the sky. They never made sense; the hidden message remained a mystery to me.

Restless and tired of staring at the ceiling about my bed, I showered and went for a jog. It had been ages since I took a carefree run, and though it would hardly be carefree, I was sure the run would do me some good. I'd packed more than enough workout gear when we headed for New Orleans. It just made sense that I would spend a lot of time training, which was exactly the case.

I tiptoed down the hall past the cracked door,

where Maggie snored so loudly if I didn't know better, I would have assumed there was a man in her room. Down the stairs, I tiptoed to avoid any noise from the creaky wood. Everyone was still snoozing. In the living room, Rhys and Malachi slept. Together!

Slouched across the couch, legs splayed in every direction, Malachi had his arm draped around Rhys' shoulder and they were both snoring, wide mouthed. Of course, I took a quick photo with my phone, and of course, I would torture them both with the image until the end of time.

Once out of the door, I allowed myself to laugh at the image. I looked at it again on my phone and couldn't help snickering to myself. It was a classic. Ready for my run, I headed down the stairs; at the end of the driveway was a car I didn't recognize. The car had tinted windows, but I could see there were two figures behind the dark glass. The suspense quickly ended when the driver's door opened and he stepped out.

"You came." I sighed when I saw him. Tall, dark-skinned with dreads that touched his waist, Demetrius. His deep brown eyes met mine and his full lips came to a half smile.

"Yes, you called, so we're here." He smiled more fully and looked back at the car.

"We?" Behind him, stepping out of the car was, Verena.

Verena, a girl I first met in New Orleans, a mystery woman who ran off into the night to speak to a strange man. The woman who they forced to be my guide on the Naiads Walk when I set off on the journey to get my Siren Stone. The woman who was almost my friend.

That was, until I attacked her during that journey. I hadn't seen her since. I assumed no one had, but apparently, Demetrius had found her.

"Verena," her name sparked an understanding that I hadn't had before.

During the Naiads Walk, Verena's reaction to Demetrius was so intense. I didn't realize it then, but seeing them together, I got it. She had deeper feelings for the brother, though I had thought the two knew nothing of each other. She smiled at me in her confident way, but this time there was a bit of an apology behind her eyes.

What had she done to feel that way? The apology should move in the opposite direction. There I was again, taking all the blame onto myself. I could hear Malachi in my mind scolding me for it. That had to stop. Not everything was my fault.

"Sy, we need to talk." Demetrius pulled me from my thoughts. "Is there somewhere we can go?"

"Um, yeah, everyone inside is still sleeping. I was about to go for a run, but we can make it a leisurely walk." It was hard to take my eyes away from his new companion, but I returned my attention to him.

"Perfect," He smiled.

"I'll wait here." Verena spoke and then quickly jumped back into the car.

Neither of us opposed her decision. It would be hard enough to have the conversation we both would rather avoid. It was, however, a necessary one, and having it with an audience would make it even worse. Walking together felt odd.

For the second day in a row, I returned to the wooded area that led to the bayous. Just the day before, I was there with Malachi, having a similar conversation, but I expected this one would be much more difficult. I was bonded with Demetrius. We were tied to each other, and it turned out that neither of us truly wanted it. After fifteen minutes of silent walking, Demetrius spoke.

"I'm in love with Verena." Just like that, he threw it out there.

It hurt to hear his words. The bond between us, though unwanted, was real, and his confession caused a sharp pain like a dagger in my chest. How could he love another when he was bonded to me? How could I…?

"Okay." I took a deep breath. Should I tell him about Rhys? Was it even necessary at this point? We were already on the same page. Demetrius wanted out, and so did I.

"Yes, and I want to be with her. I know it is a lot to ask of you after everything, but my heart is with her and I just want the chance to enjoy that love without guilt." He looked back to the car where Verena sat patiently waiting for our conversation to end.

"It looks like you're doing that already." They were clearly more than just friends. They were so much more, and though I didn't want that with Demetrius, I didn't like it.

"No, I mean, I want to be with her completely. I want to bond with her."

"How do you expect to do that when we're already bonded? Doesn't that go against the siren bylaws or something." The idea of being some sort of sister-wife with Verena was just about vomit inducing.

I didn't want to be bonded to him, no, but I damn sure wasn't about to sign up to be sharing him, either. What ramifications would that have? Would that mean that my bond with him would extend to her? No way was I signing up for that.

"That's true; a bond can only exist between a pair. That is why I am asking you to release me from the bond between us." The sun rose higher in the sky as his words settled in the air. He was asking me to release him from our bond. He wanted out and if he didn't think it was possible, he wouldn't have been asking.

"Is that something I can even do? I thought the bond was forever."

"A bond is like a marriage. We can undo it with a ritual."

"Well, okay then." I shrugged. Why not throw in a magical divorce on top of everything else? "How do we perform this ritual?"

"I was hoping you could ask your mother that." He admitted. "I'm not really sure how it works, either. I just know that it's possible."

"You know about my mom?"

"Yes, I know everything. We're bonded. It's pretty hard to block out something so major happening in your life." He looked away from me. "There were a lot of events I was there for, front and center."

"Really?" I blanched.

It had never occurred to me that the whole being bonded thing was a two-way connector. I had blocked him out, but I never questioned whether he had blocked me out. How much did he see and experience? Again, I thought of Rhys. Did Demetrius know? Oh God, did he experience everything that happened between Rhys and me?

"Look, don't freak out. I closed that door the moment that I felt you had. So anything outside of crazy dreams of your dad turning out to be evil, and you going in there and rescuing your mom, I am pretty much in the dark about." He smiled, knowing exactly where my thoughts were going. "It had to be something pretty intense to get through a shut door."

"How intense?"

"Okay, topic change. I know Alderic is coming. Tell me what I don't know. What's the plan?" We started walking again to get away from the awkward moment and usher the conversation in a new direction.

"We're trying to see if we can recruit some more help now. Maggie, a witch friend, put out a call for help. Roxanne, Rhys' mother, is now the new leader of the coven, so technically they're on our side. I still don't know what Alderic's plan is, or when he will attack. Our focus right now is pooling our resources and preparing as much as possible. I'm sure there will be no real warning before he strikes."

"You're right. After all of this, he is definitely going to use the element of surprise. It only makes sense."

"I guess we should try to get this whole bonding switch up thing done before he surprises us, huh?" I looked back to the house where Rhys and Malachi still slept, and Verena waited outside in the car. This was going to stir up a lot of shit, a lot of emotions that we had only just begun to deal with.

"That would probably be best, yes."

"Well, you know my mom is back there in the house. We can head back now. I'm sure everyone is already waking up. Roxanne is probably whipping up breakfast. That woman loves to cook!"

The walk back to the house was refreshing and accompanied by the lively songs of birds in the trees above us. I was glad that our conversation went so smoothly and I patted myself on the back for not once having apologized to Demetrius for what had happened between us. It wasn't my fault. If I kept telling myself that, it might eventually feel like the truth!

CHAPTER
19

"*I can perform the ceremony,*" my mother spoke. We had eaten our fill before I pulled her aside and asked her about releasing the bond between Demetrius and myself. "Sy, prepare yourself to cut what ties you to him. It's the same as choosing him; you just make the choice to end the bond with him."

"Well, then I do. I un-choose you." I said to Demetrius, who laughed. "Nothing happened. I still feel him."

"Yeah, it's not that simple. We still have to perform the actual ceremony." My mother laughed at me as well. Well, forgive a girl for hoping that, for once, something was going to be that simple. "Syrinada, you will have to replace him with another. Once a siren has been bonded, she cannot be without a mate. The only way for that to happen is for the mate to die. I assume neither of you is so desperately to be separated that you will die for this."

"You assume correctly." The merman spoke, and I paused. No, I wasn't thinking about laying my life down for the cause. What worried me, though, were the thoughts that swarmed my mind about the ramifications of our choice.

"Oh?" I looked at my fingers.

Why couldn't we just be free of the bond altogether, as if we'd never bonded in the first place? Neither of us wanted it, so why did I have to transfer that unwanted responsibility to someone else? There was only one other merman around, the brother of the one that I was disconnecting from. Things were just getting better and now this was about to fuck it all up!

"Okay, we must do this quickly. An unbonded siren is a vulnerable one, especially when she is with her full power." She stood and grabbed two candles from the drawer of the table next to the entrance and headed for the living room. "I don't think I have to express why that would be a bad thing, especially now. Let's go."

"Now?" I stared at her. Demetrius had already stood and was following her out of the hall. Shit, I just wanted to go for a morning jog!

"Everyone, please gather!" My mother called out as she walked through the halls.

"What's going on?" Maggie, who had napped on her full stomach, rolled over onto the couch to find us all standing over her.

"We're about to perform a ceremony. Syrinada is to dissolve the bond with her current mate, Demetrius. Her bond will move to another, so that Demetrius can join with his true love, Verena." She nodded at Verena, who stood behind Demetrius with a proud and anxious smile on her face.

Even though I was still wary of the process, seeing how the two of them lit up at the idea made it all worth it. Hell, I was already in a shitty situation. What's a little transference?

"Everyone, please spread out, make a circle. Rhys, Malachi, if you can push the sofa back out of the way. We must do this inside. If Alderic senses that this is happening, he can use it to his advantage, so we must do quickly this." She handed a candle to Demetrius and one to me.

Everyone moved into his or her places as directed by my mother. To my right were Ebon and Roxanne, and to my left was Maggie. At the head of the circle was my mother. Directly across from me is Demetrius. To his right was Verena, who held his hand. Malachi stood to the left of Verena, and Rhys to the right of Demetrius.

"This is a ceremony of transference. These two have relinquished their bond and have chosen instead to bond with those who hold their heart." My mother held the attention of the room.

I couldn't help but look at Malachi, whose face lit up, and then at Rhys, who deflated. My heart ached. This could not be happening again.

"Demetrius Denali," she handed him a candle which lit when he took it. "And Syrinada Sania." The same happened when I took the candle from her. "You two are bonded now, but wish to separate. Step forward towards one another." We did as instructed and she looked at Demetrius. "Repeat after me. I Demetrius Denali releases you, Syrinada Sania, from the bond of mates and accept this new bond into my heart."

Nervously, Demetrius looked at me and then back over his shoulder at Verena, who still held his hand. He repeated her words, and each one left me feeling more empty, more alone, and more afraid. When he was done, his candle went out, and I felt the reverberation of that darkness inside of my chest. How could I feel so empty? I could I feel so broken without him? I didn't even want him!

"Syrinada, now it is your turn." My mother nodded to me.

"I-" I paused, and looked around the room, and avoided the two who stared so intently at me.

"Baby, just close your eyes and let your heart do

the talking. This is a genuine bond. Your mate will show himself to you." Everyone around me inhaled at the same time and held their breath while I played my part in the ceremony.

I inhaled deeply and closed my eyes to repeat the words, swapping his name for my own. "I Syrinada Sania release you, Demetrius Denali, from the bond of mates and accept this new bond into my heart." The power of the shift was so immense that everyone in the room gasped. When I opened my eyes, my flame had also gone out.

"Lay your eyes on the one who your heart belongs to, your true mate, and the flame will reemerge." My mother spoke. Demetrius turned to Verena and his candle relit its blaze, now brighter and stronger than it was before. He pulled her into his arms, holding the candle at a safe distance, and kissed her deeply. I smiled at the sight. That image was worth it all.

"Syrinada," my mother urged. "You must complete the transfer; you cannot leave the bond broken."

"I know, I understand." I swept my eyes from the new couple's smiling face to the floor, working up the nerve to face this new problem. When I raised my eyes, I took toward an eager Malachi. I smiled slightly, and he beamed.

"It's not working." Maggie spoke after a few moments passed. My candle remained unlit.

"That's because he isn't her true mate." My mother whispered, and I looked at her. She could sense the fear that I had. Not because of what it meant about the person who was really meant to be my mate, but because of the backlash it would cause.

"What do you mean?" Malachi asked, his heartbreak disturbing the smooth tenor of his voice.

"Syrinada," my mother nodded to me and I took another deep breath, closed my eyes, and allowed my heart to lead me.

When I opened my eyes, the candle burst into a bright flame that illuminated my sight. In front of me stood the man I loved. He stood in a halo of light that only I could see, the man who held my heart from the moment we met.

"It's you." I smiled and walked towards the one who lit my heart aflame. "Rhys."

He stared at me with a hungry smile and pulled me into his arms. "How can this be?"

"The heart chooses what it wants." My mother responded simply.

Rhys kissed me, and my chest warmed. I tightened my arms around his neck. Though I was happier than I'd been in a long time, in the back of my mind was the concern for Malachi, but it was barely there. The feeling of completion, the feeling of being with Rhys, was engulfing. When our lips parted, I turned to see everyone watching us. Malachi stared at the floor to avoid looking at me. Before the sound of his name could cross my lips, he left the room and punched a hole in the door's frame on his way out.

CHAPTER
20

"*Malachi, let her go for your own peace of mind.* You can't keep holding on to some hope that she will come back to you." Demetrius offered unwelcomed advice to his younger brother.

Listening in on their conversation may have been wrong, but I couldn't help it. I stood in the shadows by the door, hoping Demetrius could ease his brother's mind. Malachi had left the house for a while after he left an imprint of his fist on Roxanne's wall. No one could find him, but for whatever reason, he returned.

He stood on the front porch, refusing to come back inside. Instead of trying to convince him to come in, Demetrius joined him and tried to speak to him about what he was going through. They left the door open just a crack, and I stood on the other side and held my breath as they spoke.

"I know, but he is a fucking witch!" Malachi shouted, and the pain in his voice cut right through me. "This isn't right. She doesn't belong with him. That's not how this is supposed to work!"

"Apparently, she does. Yes, he is a witch, but he is also a powerful one. He is someone who has connected with her and helped her through some pretty difficult shit." Demetrius explained. "Remember that Syrinada is half witch. That side of her plays an important part in how this all works out. She isn't like us. Maybe there is something he can give her that neither of us can."

As difficult as the words were to say, Demetrius knew his brother needed to hear them. I sighed, happy that I wasn't the one to say them. It sounded better coming from someone who could understand how he felt.

"I just, man, I thought," He growled and hit something; I'm assuming it was the wall next to the door by the way the frame shook. Despite the shock, I didn't give up my position. "I feel like such a fucking idiot, D!"

"I know what you thought, but this isn't that. It never will be, and you have to move on with your life."

"How?" It sounded as if he was holding back tears. He paused for a long moment. "How am I supposed to just let go of a lifetime of loving that woman? How do I just move on from giving every damn part of what I am, my heart and soul, to her? She calls and I come. It's not because I have to, we both know that!

"There is no bond between us. Which means there was nothing obligating me to do a damn thing for her! But I did it anyway. Anything she asked of me, I was there. It's because I can't not want to be near her. I am incapable of turning away from her, no matter how bad it hurts to face her. She owns every bit of me. Even the fucking demon couldn't break free of her hold!"

"What do you mean?" Demetrius asked, his tone sharing the same edge of concern I felt.

"I set him free. Hell, I was ready to accept that evil into my life if it meant not having to feel this pain. Her voice wouldn't leave my head. I kept hearing her, calling for me and then feeling her pull back; she regretted needing me, wanting me.

"You don't know what that feels like. No matter what I did, she was there. I couldn't block her out then, and I can't now. I have sworn my life to protecting her, to caring for her. Without hesitation, I promised all that I am to her, and she wants none of me! So what exactly do you expect me to do, brother? How am I just supposed to let her go when she is so deeply imbedded into who I am now?"

"I don't know." Demetrius' tone was calm, level; he couldn't get emotional when dealing with a brother who was already on the edge. "I wish I could tell you how to let this go. I wish that there were some way to just take it from you. There is nothing I can do for you and it kills me, but I don't want to watch you torture yourself over this anymore."

"Malachi," Taking my cue, I called his name as I stepped out onto the porch.

There was nothing that Demetrius could do or say that would fix anything. Malachi's anger wasn't rooted in his relationship with his brother. His problem was with me and if he was ever to get closure, I had to give him the opportunity to deal with it head on.

"Can we have a moment alone, please?" I asked, looking at Demetrius because I didn't think his brother would agree.

"Yeah," Demetrius paused and waited for confirmation from his brother before leaving us alone.

"I'm sorry." I placed my hands on the banister. The sun had just set and the night's breeze cut the through the humidity the hot day left behind.

"I told you before to stop apologizing to me. It fixes nothing." He kept his distance from me and even took a step further away, putting him closer to the stairs. Would he make a run for it?

"What would you have me say?" I looked at him even though he tried avoiding eye contact. "How am I supposed to address this if not with an apology? You've been there for me for so long, even before I knew you were. There is no way I could have ever known what would come of this. You can't think that I would have ever asked you to come here if I'd expected anything like this to happen. Rhys and I," Malachi lifted his hand to stop me from continuing.

"Sy, just please don't," he dropped his shoulders and sighed. "I can't take another apology. I don't want it."

"You're right; I can't apologize to you for this. I realize you are hurting, but this, like so much else that has happened to me, is outside of my control."

"I know that, I just... why not me? Why Demetrius? Why Rhys? Why is it everyone else but me?" Deciding that the distance was no longer necessary, he stepped to me, grabbed me by the shoulders gently, and peered into my eyes as if searching my soul for a last ember of hope.

"I have loved you my entire life. Before I knew what love meant, I felt this pull towards you. Even now, as I allow this demon in me to roam free, hoping he will eliminate the love I have for you, it is still there. It burns. This want, this desire to be everything you need me to be. Yet, you want nothing of me. You chose Demetrius, and I understood it was a way to dodge something you weren't ready to face. It hurt, but I understood it and I came to terms with it. Now I see you do want it. You want it all, just not with me."

"Malachi-"

"Let me finish, please. How am I supposed to move forward from this? How am I supposed to live my life knowing that you will never be mine? I have spent my entire life protecting that very idea, that you would come into your own and you would take your place at my side."

"It's that!" I pulled away from him.

I had been so busy trying to make him feel better for what I had done to him, but not once did I stop to make him face what he had done to me. Malachi was playing the victim, and it was time for that to end.

"That right there. You have so much expectation, so many things that you already had in your mind, long before I ever knew you even existed. Can you even understand how overwhelming and frustrating it is for me? How could I ever know if what you felt for me was really for me? How am I supposed to be sure that the reason you want to be with me now isn't just a result of your believing for so long that we belonged together?"

Malachi tried to turn away from me, but I stepped back into his view. I wouldn't let him run from this. He didn't want apologies, fine, but he wouldn't stop me from speaking my truth.

"It was too much pressure!" I cried out. "Rhys asks nothing of me. Not now, not from the moment we met.

He's expected nothing from me. Malachi, you, though I know it was not your intention; you requested the world from me. For me to be brave, strong, and love you, even though I had lost sight of who and what I was. How could I ever make that commitment to you or anyone else? How was that fair to me?"

I waited for him to answer me. Sounds of the night filled the void between us. Chirps and squeaks of creatures echoed in the night. He said nothing, only tried to avoid looking at me. So I continued. And I would continue talking until he answered me.

"I'm so tired of saying this to you and everyone else, but I never wanted to hurt you. Hell, you saw how much it took for me to stop fighting against all of this. That right there, your expectation, was a big part of the reason I fought so hard for things not to change! This transition has brought a shit storm into my life and I am just trying to get through it. I understand if you decide not to stick around and help us with this. No one will blame you for walking away."

He was right, I shouldn't have been apologizing, and I didn't owe him one. What we both needed was closure: not only so that he could heal, but so that I could as well.

"Malachi, I have to let this go, this guilt for the pain that I have caused you, however unintentional it may have been. I have to focus on what is happening now. If you want to talk about this, to have an open and honest discussion, we can do that. We can do that as long and as often as you need to until you can move on.

"What I won't do is continue to beat myself up over this, because for the first time in a very long time, something in my life feels right. I refuse to question that feeling. I wish it wasn't at the expense of your feelings, but I need this and I will let nothing disrupt that."

"I get that, I really do, but I need you to understand something for me." Malachi finally spoke but still kept his eyes away from mine. "My heart is broken. Right now, I feel like someone has ripped my soul from me. Yes, I know that you never meant to cause this, just as I never meant to put so much pressure on you. That doesn't change the fact that the pain is still there."

He finally looked at me and I wished he hadn't because I saw it all. The pain, the sorrow, the emptiness. That was why he left the way he did. Something was missing inside of him. Something that I couldn't give back to him. I remained quiet, this time letting him speak his truth.

"On some level," he continued. "Even if time takes away what I feel now, I will always belong to you, even though it's clear that you wish that weren't true. What is true is that you will never belong to me. I am incapable of bonding with another. Believe me, I have tried. It was the first thing I tried after I realized not even my demonic side could outrun you. Even when I found someone who wanted me, and chose me, it didn't work because of you. There is now, there always was and forever will be, only you."

"Malachi,"

"I need time away from you. Demetrius will keep me informed and I will be there when you need me. Whenever you call me, I will come." He turned away from me and headed down the stairs, but paused for a moment and without turning back to look at me. "After this is over, after we go our separate ways, please do me a favor. Don't call on me."

Malachi stepped from the porch and into the blanket of darkness that surrounded the house. I wanted to follow him, make everything okay again, but I knew that there was no way to accomplish that. Regardless of my intentions, he was hurting, and he needed to figure out a way to heal. Tears fell down my cheeks as I mourned for my friend. Our relationship would never be the same.

"Are you okay?" Rhys' gentle voice wrapped around me as his arms did the same. Cocooned in his warmth and lulled by his love, I sobbed.

"I hurt him. I can never undo the pain I have caused him." My head was on his shoulder. He tightened his hold around me and laid his head atop mine.

"No one expects you to."

"It isn't fair." I sobbed. "Why does my finding my happiness mean that he must lose his forever?"

"I wouldn't say forever. Only time can tell that." Rhys kissed the top of my head. "I'm sure there's more in store for the brooding merman."

CHAPTER
21

It was easier to leave, and our absence was an absolute necessity. Even with Malachi away from the house, it was too damn crowded. There was no way that I could go back inside the house after watching Malachi walk away.

Every single person inside those walls would pounce with their own intrusive agendas as soon as the door opened. Some would grill me about the new bond with Rhys. Maggie, and others, would ask about Malachi, my mother, and Demetrius. They would want to know specifically what I said and how he reacted. How could I rehash everything that happened with him when it still hurt so much to think about? The healing had begun, but it was far from over.

"Rhys?" still standing on the porch, I turned my head and pressed my lips against his neck. He was the only person I wanted to be near.

"Yes," he returned my affection with a kiss on my cheek.

"Please, get me out of here. Just take me away, even if it's only for one night. I know there is so much that needs to be done, but I really need to get away. It's just too much."

Placing his hand on my shoulder, he turned my body towards him. When he lifted my chin, he saw the heartache in my eyes. He witnessed my pain, my unhappiness, and my fear. I was weak and depressed, and with the strength of our new bond, there wasn't enough energy left to sustain the barrier I usually kept in place to keep my emotions hidden.

I closed my eyes because it helped. It helped to block out some of the hurt. It helped me convince myself that I wasn't as tired or as beaten up as I felt. Rhys said nothing, but he granted my wish. Without opening my eyes to confirm, I knew he had used his magic to take us away.

Gone away from the sticky night air and the sound of flies buzzing nearby. In its place now, the struggling hum of an overused air conditioner and the smell of partially burned wood. A smile that spread across my face when I recognized the familiar feel of our new location.

"I see they still haven't fixed that door." The image of the front door of the average sized apartment, sitting slightly off its hinges, reminded me of our first introduction to Maggie, the fire throwing witch bitch.

I laughed at the not so distant memory of Rhys' reaction to finding out that the one who blew off that door would join our little crusade. It was a good thing she was on our side.

"Yeah, I guess I forgot to put in that maintenance request with the whole, running from the evil witch coven thing." He laughed.

"It feels so good to be back here. Is that crazy?" I bent down to pick up a throw pillow and put it back on the sofa where it belonged. "I mean, this was our hideout. We were on the run, but I liked it here."

"I see nothing crazy about that." My back was to him, but I could hear the smile in his voice.

"I miss the peace of this place. I miss waking up to breakfast in bed and how normal things felt. It was almost like none of that other stuff existed." I sighed, looking around the room and watching memories of our time there play out. "I got to just... be, again. Good food, rest, and great company. I miss it."

"I miss bringing you breakfast in bed, and lunch, and dinner." He smiled and pulled me back into his arms to kiss me. "Stay here. I like you being right here. Close to me."

"Yeah?" I smirked and pretended to pull away, but he pulled me back again.

"Yes." He kissed my face and my cheeks lifted against the gentle pressure.

"So tell me, what else do you miss?" I ran my fingertips across the back of his neck.

"I miss the life you brought to this place. Just look at it, all the plants have died."

He was right. I hadn't noticed at first, but all the plants that we'd collected were brown and withered. Thir fallen leaves littered the hardwood floors and table tops.

"That's so sad." I pulled away from him and gave my attention to the decaying plant life.

Reluctantly, he let me go and watched as I crossed the room. I reached out to touch the tip of an aloe plant and called to the life inside of it. It was still there; it was dim, but there was just enough to grab hold of. I closed my eyes asked for it to come back to me. To allow me to see its beauty once more.

Slowly, spreading from the place where my fingertip made contact, life. The undesirable brown became a vibrant green, and the color reached down the length of the petal and stretched to the root of the plant. Moments later, it was alive again. Languid limbs stretched proudly towards the ceiling.

"You are so amazing. Just stop and look at this. Look at what you've just done."

One by one, the others perked up as well. Flowers bloomed again, and rubber plants, which were never meant to die, bounced back to life. My favorite, the bamboo, not only did it return to me but also it grew further, as if reaching out to hug me. I smiled at the awesomeness of it all.

"I still feel like I don't know what I am doing most of the time." I looked at Rhys. "The power I have. Sometimes it's just so chaotic. But this, I know this. This is who I am."

"And yet, even with the chaos you struggle to understand, you still leave us all in awe. You just breathed life into something once without it. Do you know how amazing that is?"

"I know how amazing it feels. To finally see some value in this situation, something positive. I hope that it's enough to keep everyone safe. That's what I've worried about the most. That I wouldn't be able to protect those that I care so much for. My mom, you, everyone. It's still not completely clear to me how, but now I feel like I can."

"Syrinada, I don't want you to worry about me. Not now, and definitely not when it comes time to face

Alderic."

"I will try, but I'm not sure how I'm actually supposed to accomplish that." I returned to his side and held out my hand for him to hold.

"I want you to stop just for a moment. Stop and think of nothing at all. Can you do that?" He pulled me close to him and lifted my hand to place his lips softly at the edge of my knuckles.

"I've tried. It doesn't exactly work." It was all I did. I tried so hard to eliminate the constant noise, the echoes of my worries. No method had worked.

"Okay, think of this." His lips moved, traveled across the back of my hand, up my arm, peppered my neck in soft flutters, and finally claimed my lips.

"That's nice." I smiled against the full borders of his mouth.

"Syrinada," he whispered my name as his hands grabbed my waist and brought the forms of our bodies to meet.

"Yes, Rhys?"

"Think of nothing but the feel of me. My lips against yours." He pressed his lips to mine again. "Against the flesh of your neck." He demonstrated. "My hands touching your back and bringing you closer to me." Again, his actions authenticated his words.

"Yes." My core warmed and my siren rejoiced. This was like no other encounter. He was mine, and the bond between us was on fire.

"How does it feel?" His breath brushed against my skin as he called my mind to focus.

"It feels amazing, Rhys. You feel amazing." I sighed, pressing my body closer to his.

"Think of nothing, but this, let everything else go. It is only you and me."

"Rhys," his name was a breathy echo of the symphony inside my mind.

"Yes, Syrinada?"

"I want you." I declared.

"Syrinada, I am right here, and I am yours." He lifted me into his arms and carried me to the bedroom.

Even though we'd been together before, this time, back in our hideaway, felt like the first time. It felt like the first time he had ever laid his eyes on me. The first time he'd ever looked at me with hunger and desire. It was the first time he'd removed my clothes, or the bare skin of his chest had pressed against my own. Despite what I knew, it felt like the first time my body had ever accepted another.

Rhys took his time with that first time. Opening the

curtains so that the stars could light the room, he looked at me, nude, laying across the bed, and admired what he knew belonged to him. His silent claim, his mark on me, I welcomed it. No other had proven more deserving of that title. Rhys was my mate.

My mate crossed the room and stripped away his own clothing, leaving layers of fabric on the floor. He slowly crawled up the bed, kissing my ankle, and rubbing the scruff of his unshaven face against my calf. He drew slow licks across the flesh of my inner thigh until his lips met my sweet spot.

Head between my thighs, he kissed me; he fed from me and drank in my juices. As he satisfied his thirst, my head spun with each pass of his tongue, each suckling of my clit, and each delve inside. His fingers assisted his efforts; I clutched the sheets as he coaxed me, bringing me closer and closer to orgasm.

"Oh, my... Rhys!" I cried out in sweet, deliciously intense ecstasy.

Before my climax could fully end, he lifted me by my bare ass; fingers kept me open to his arrival, and with an agonizing yet intoxicatingly slow pace, positioned me on his throbbing arousal. With each inch of him that merged with me. I felt power; I felt full, and I felt strength.

Rhys felt it too; he called out my name once he'd entered me as far as he could go and gripped my waist.

I took over, twirled my hips slowly, and enjoyed the sheer look of pleasure on his face. I moved his hands to cup my breast as I continued to work my motion on him. Muscles squeezed within me, tightened my hold on him, and pushed him closer to his own eruption.

He would not give in to me. As hard as I tried, Rhys held on. He regained control. My mate flipped me in one smooth motion onto my knees and entered me fully from behind. This time there was no smooth, tantalizingly torturous entrance. He thrust inside of me, wrapped one hand in my hair, and guided my hips with the other.

I gave into him. My legs trembled and my arms gave out as I dropped to my chest. I arched my back and allowed him full access. He pushed down on me, pushed deeper into me, and as the length of him reached my limit, I exploded. He grabbed my ass and pulled out; with one deep and powerful thrust, Rhys gave himself to me. His heat throbbed between my walls as he unloaded into me and I accepted every bit of him.

Everything felt different, stronger. Our connection reinforced my power, as it had never been before. When he touched me, pulled me into him as we lay in our afterglow, I felt sexy and strong. The feeling wasn't just superficial. It reached deep into my core, caressed my soul, and milked the very power that was harnessed within me.

Finally, my mind was silent; the world was quiet,

except for the soft tremble at my neck caused by the gentle snoring of my lover. Smiling with echoes of my pleasure, completely satisfied, I pulled his arm tighter around me, and closed my eyes.

~*~

The morning brought the warmth of the sun through the windows and the smell of life. The plants in the apartment thrived and filled the air with their herbaceous fragrance. I smiled languidly as Rhys buried his face in my hair and pulled me tighter against his body.

"Good morning." His voice was thick with the residue of his sleep. He kissed my shoulder and flashed his best lazy smile.

"Good morning," I rolled so I could face him fully. "It's so nice, waking up next to you."

"I'm glad you like it. I plan to make it a standard activity." He brushed the stray hairs from my face and kissed me softly. "How are you feeling?"

"I'm feeling much better, starving, but much better." I rubbed my stomach and looked at him with pleading eyes.

It had been so long since he'd cooked for me. From the moment we stepped foot in Roxanne's home, she was the chef and he the patron. Her food was delicious, but something about having him in the kitchen, cooking for me, made the food taste so much better!

"I can make us something, though I'm sure everything in that fridge is spoiled beyond recognition." He laughed and scrunched up his nose.

I thought of the smell that would no doubt explode into the apartment the moment he opened the door and frowned. The fragrance of the plants and flowers that filled the air was definitely preferred. I breathed it all in again and felt their life coming to me. "On second thought, maybe we can go out to eat."

"Mmm, go out. I wish." He lifted his arms above his head and stretched his body. The sunlight gave his flesh a warm glow and highlighted the muscles beneath the skin. His dark skin contrasted beautifully with my own. I loved studying the difference between our tones and, even more so, witnessing them blending together when we made love.

"Why wish it? Let's do it!" I sat up in the bed and looked out of the window.

Down on the street, I could see all the people who were hustling off to enjoy his or her day. I wanted to join them, to be a part of the crowded streets and jammed restaurants. I wanted to fade into the background of everyday life.

"We have to get back." Warmth spread along my

back as he touched my skin and massaged it, gradually increasing in pressure.

This man was evil! How dare he massage me into facing reality!

"Can't we play hooky for just a while longer?" Pout face on, I peered over my shoulder at him. It wouldn't work, but it would make him smile.

"No, unfortunately." Score, there was my smile and then came the blow. "I think it's best that we head back now. We still don't know what your father is planning or when he will set off whatever he is cooking up. What we do know is that we don't want to be away when it happens."

"Whelp, there goes my bubbly mood." I flopped back onto the bed in the most dramatic fashion I could muster up and crushed his hand beneath me.

"I'm sorry; I just think it's best we play it safe."

"No, you're right. We should play it safe. It's just nice to pretend now and then that I have the option of not being responsible."

"I know. Soon this will all be behind us and then we will lounge around and eat out whenever our hearts desire." With some effort, he freed his arm from beneath me and moved from the bed. It was time to go.

"Steak? Can we go out for steak?" My eyes followed

him and with each piece of clothing that returned to his body, reality set in that much more.

"Absolutely, anything you want." That smile, that heart-melting smile, took the fight out of me completely. He was right.

"Sounds wonderful." I smacked the mattress and cursed the ceiling. Back to reality.

CHAPTER 22

It was clear even before we made it back to Roxanne's home in New Orleans that something wasn't right. In my absence, something had gone terribly wrong inside the house.

The heaviness of evil pulled me down long before my feet could touch the ground. Alderic had done something. His energy lingered there, fresh and toxic. Whatever he did, it was no small thing, but it targeted the house and left residual magic that was still at work.

The moment my feet hit the porch, I took off. I pushed the door aside and followed the trail of evil. It was a disgusting feeling, and the closer I got to it, the sicker I felt. My heart dropped as I realized where the path led me. Up the stairs and across the hall from my room, the room that once was Rhys', the room that now belonged to my mother.

"What happened?" I asked as I pushed by Ebon and Roxanne, who stood at her bedside. My mother lay frozen on her bed. Eyes wide in terror, she stared at the ceiling. What was she looking at? What was she experiencing?

"I'm not sure. I was heading down to get breakfast started and thought I'd peek in on her. When she didn't answer after I called her name a few times, I came in and found her like this." Roxanne laid her hand on my shoulder. "We've tried everything to wake her, to pull her from this. Nothing has worked."

"What's wrong?" Rhys caught up to me and replaced his mother behind me. He laid his hands on my shoulders as Roxanne gave him the same recap of the events.

"I can fix this." The words left my mouth, even though I wasn't sure they were true.

There was so much more I had already accomplished with even less knowledge or understanding. This had to be within my abilities.

"Are you sure?" Maggie Ebon asked. "I'm not sure what this is, but it's powerful."

"Yes, I've undone his magic before." I answered with more confidence than I should have. "I can do it again. He can't have her."

Still, I pressed the palms of my hands firmly against my mother's chest and forehead. Her skin was ice cold. Whatever was happening, I had little time to stop it. I closed my eyes and asked for Rhys to remain as he was. His touch was strengthening, and I didn't know how much of me it would take to set her free.

With my mind, I reached across the barrier put in place by my father and called to my mother.

Come to me, find my voice, and return to me.

I could feel her stirring inside. His hold wasn't as strong as it could have been. He didn't mean for it to be. This was only happening because he wanted to prove a point to me. Again, I stretched my energy toward her until I found a firm hold. Linked, I pulled with all that it took to bring her back. Her body relaxed and her eyes shut for a moment before her mind fully returned to her.

"Syrinada," she smiled in a manner that gave me déjà vu.

"Mom," I leaned down to wrap my arms around her. She was weak, but I needed to feel the life within her.

"You saved me, again." Her voice was small and frail. What had he done to her mind?

"Yeah, let's try not to make a habit of it. I need you to be okay." I kissed her cheek. "Can you tell me what happened?"

"It felt like just another odd dream, one of those things where everything seems normal, but it isn't, and you just can't quite put your finger on it. I've been having them since I woke up, but this one lasted for so long." My mother slowly explained her experience. "I wanted to wake up, but I couldn't. Then, he was there, and I knew it was really him. He told me that the time of my return was ending. Everything stopped. I tried to wake up, to escape him, but I was too late. He had me again."

"Okay, well, he doesn't have you anymore. You're here. Safe. Try to get some rest." I helped her get comfortable before turning to the small witch who held the most power in the house. "Ebon, is there anything you can do to protect her from this happening again?"

"I can try a protection spell, but there is no promise that it will work, not with their lives being linked how they are." She moved to stand at the head of the bed and placed her hand on my mother's forehead. "I will do all that I can."

"Thank you. Please do whatever it takes." I turned to Rhys' mother, who watched my mother with worried eyes. "Roxanne, if you could help her, lend your power?"

"Absolutely." She smiled at my mother lovingly. "I would do anything for my friend."

"He is doing this to prove a point." Rhys spoke in hushed tones as we walked across the hall to my bedroom.

"What do you mean?" I pushed the door closed. It was the same feeling I got, but his insight was valuable. Rhys knew my father better than anyone. If there were a message behind the madness, he would be the one to see it.

"He is showing us he can hurt us, even if defeated. His death will be her death. Imagine the state of mind he is in. If she is hurting this badly, so is he."

"He is hurting?" I looked over my shoulder back to the bedroom where they worked on my mother.

"Yes, their lives are one; her pain is his as well. Just think of what type of magic it took to keep him awake while she slept, frozen. I have been thinking about this since we found out about the link between the two of them." Rhys moved to the desk by the window, took out pen and paper, and he started drawing symbols and lines linking my mother's name to my father's.

"Alderic is wielding power far beyond anything he should be capable of. It makes sense, looking back on my time there with him. He was always going on about the time. Then he would get a call, and next thing I knew, he was running off. That was the only reason he showed me how to come and go on my own. Tell me, who would have been calling?"

"I don't know." I shrugged. "Maybe he was working with someone?"

"I don't think so." He drew a spiral in the center of the page. "I think he was on a cycle. And whenever he had to run off, it was because he needed to do whatever it took to keep him from falling into a deep sleep, just like your mother."

"You're right. It makes so much sense now." Though his epiphany brought more clarity to our situation, it also brought up another problem for us to solve.

"Alderic wants us to think he is in control, but I don't think he is." Rhys put the pen down and waited for me to process what he said.

It went without saying that the plan was to rid the world of Alderic. Stripping him of his powers wouldn't be enough; he'd already proven that he could get powers that didn't belong to him. Having to face possibly killing my father was horrible enough, but with his life directly connected to my mother's, there was no way to kill him without killing her as well. There was no way I'd be able to do that.

~*~

"Is there a way that we can remove the link between them?" Rhys spoke about my mother to the group that had gathered around the dining table.

That room had quickly become our headquarters whenever something needed to be discussed. Ebon and Roxanne had finally gotten my mother the protection she needed to rest. She lay in her bed, undisturbed; I kept my mind on her.

While listening to the conversation, I monitored the energy in the home. I had to be sure Alderic hadn't returned to her. She couldn't be left defenseless, and we couldn't know he wouldn't try to hurt her again. I felt nothing and hoped Rhys was right. Alderic would need the same time to recover as she did. She was free of his tyranny, for the time being.

"He is going to come at us with all that he has, and we need to be sure that we can face him and take him down. We all know that he will never stop." Rhys continued. "After all that he has gone through, the time that he has invested in getting this far, I can't see him simply giving up now."

"I don't know." Roxanne looked at us with somber eyes. "It took the borrowed magic of a really powerful witch to perform the spell that binds them; it was with her help that I could do it. I'm stronger than I was then, but I doubt I have the strength it would take to do it alone."

"Well, who was she? Maybe we can help figure this all out. Someone in her lineage, maybe? Sometimes, power doesn't go over into the next world, it passes on." Maggie was already working out how to find the long-lost descendant. "If she was part of this coven, her family is likely still around."

"Her name was Eloise and as far as I know, she had no other family. It was just her, her mother, and her sister." Roxannes told us between sips of her tea. "Her mother died long before I ever found out about her and no one ever knew what happened to her sister. There was a lot of speculation, but of course nothing based on fact."

"Eloise?" Ebon spoke this time. She had been a quiet observer of our conversation, but the name triggered something. At the head of the table that was usually covered with food, she looked to Roxanne for confirmation of the name.

"Yes, it wasn't easy to find her, but when I did, she was so welcoming. She helped me without questioning my motives or my end game. It was like she knew I would come."

"She helped you do this?" Ebon contemplated the information carefully.

I leaned forward, trying to read the ghost's energy. The air around her body charged, then settled. What did it mean? Was Eloise some missing key? Whatever it was, as long as it helped keep my mother safe, I was all for it.

"Yes, she said it was her duty and that one day I

would understand why." Roxanne sat just left of Ebon and waited like the rest of us to hear what she had to say.

"Well, it would seem today is that day." She smiled and laughed. "I can't believe I didn't put that together."

"What do you mean?" I asked hopefully. "Put what together?"

"Eloise, she was special to me." Ebon looked me in the eye. "My darling little sister. It was so hard to walk away from her."

"You're Eloise's older sister?" Roxanne gasped, then started rambling. "I have heard so many stories about you; all of them seemed so farfetched. No one ever seemed to know your name; most didn't believe that you actually even existed."

"I am sure there is a bit of truth to most of the stories. Few people knew of my existence. It was my mother's effort to keep me safe. She tried," Ebon shook her head as something dark passed through her mind. "They found us anyway. I am who I say I am, and if it was Eloise's power that sealed the bond on this spell, it is mine that will unlock it."

"You would do that?" My mother could be saved if Ebon would help. She'd already come to aid us in stopping my father, but how far would that help go?

"It would seem that was always my sister's intention and whether or not she is here, Eloise always gets her way." She smiled as she reflected on a personal thought. "I was drawn here. The others did not agree with my involvement, but it was something that I couldn't avoid. Eventually, with reluctance, they gave into the idea. Now I know why I felt the need to be here with you. Eloise's magic is a part of this, and her magic is a part of me."

"You can undo this? That is great. You reverse the spell, and we can deal with Alderic." Rhys turned to me. "We need to sit down and come up with an exact plan; we can't come at this on the fly. He has thought through every moment, and we need to get ahead of him."

"There is a lot to do." Ebon took over the conversation again and handed out instructions. "Roxanne, you must remember the spell to its exact order. Once you provide that to me, I can begin working on a counter spell. We must act quickly. Alderic will strike soon." She changed her focus as she stood from her seat to walk around the table to Maggie.

"Margaret, you need to get the covens ready. Prepare them for what is coming." Ebon stood by Maggie's side and looked into her eyes. "I'm so sorry, child." She lifted a finger to touch Maggie on the forehead.

The young witch's eyes rolled into the back of her head and she shook as Ebon filled her mind with images. Dark images that Maggie would never give me or anyone else at the table, more than vague explanations of. Rhys grabbed my hand because he recognized my need to help her and his touch reminded me that Ebon was friend, not foe.

The room felt smaller, its homey feel turned into more of a restraint as time moved slowly forward. Maggie sobbed deeply and wrapped her arms around herself as the small finger dropped away from her forehead.

"Oh," Maggie looked at me with tear-filled eyes, and her body still trembled. "I will do whatever it takes."

"What did you show her?" Secrets were not okay with me, secrets were lies. Whatever Maggie saw, we all needed to see. We needed to know what we were up against.

"Only a possibility, nothing that is set in stone," Ebon answered me, then looked at Maggie again. "Nothing that cannot be changed."

"Maggie," Roxanne spoke gently and considered the fragile state Maggie appeared to be in. "Do you think you can perform the spell again, to help me remember? That spell was not one I kept on hand. I didn't think that I would ever have a need or a means for working that magic again." It would have been nice if Ebon had waited to fry Maggie's brain. Hell, it would have been better had she not done it at all, but there was no undoing what was already done.

"Yes, of course. We can get started right away." she stood from the table.

"Are you sure you don't want to take a moment?" Rhys was concerned about her, as we all were. He let my hand go and stood to assist her if she needed.

"I'm fine. My brain has been through worse." She smiled, but it wasn't full and her voice didn't hold her usual spunk or quirk. "Roxanne, whenever you're ready."

"At least let me help you to the other room." Again, Rhys was there for her.

"If you insist," she turned to me and, with a sly eye and a slight lift of her lips, said, "Such a charmer you have here. You better take good care of him, or someone may try to snatch him up!"

I forced a smile across my face. Using humor to cover hurt was not her strongest talent.

"What did you show her?" I turned to Ebon again once they were out of earshot.

"What she needed to see. If I meant it for you to know, you would." Ebon said nothing else on the matter.

I wanted to protest her, to tell her she was playing with our lives, but it would make no difference. She wouldn't tell me. Instead of arguing and costing us more time, I eased back into my chair and listened as she addressed Roxanne.

"You need to get to work. I will gather the basic ingredients that Eloise used in all of her spells and rituals, which will give us a head start. I'm sure there will be at least one or two more items that I will need. That is what you need to figure out, also the exact words she used for the incantation."

"Yes, I will get started right away." Both women left the room, leaving me to my own thoughts.

"You okay?" Rhys returned as Demetrius and Verena, the silent parties, left behind the two witches.

I had almost forgotten they were in the room. The two sat silent the entire meeting. Demetrius would report back to Malachi, whatever he needed to know.

"Yes, just checking in on mom again." I looked up at him. "She is still resting peacefully."

"You just found out that we can save her, yet you don't look happy." Rhys pulled up the chair next to me and sat down.

"What is there to be happy about? Yes, my mom will be okay, but will everyone else? Hell, this doesn't even ensure that we can keep her safe. It's just one hurdle in the obstacle course from hell and we haven't officially conquered it yet. There's nothing to be excited about." I leaned on the table with my elbows and folded my hands beneath my chin. "It is just so much to take in, you know?

It just keeps coming!"

"What can I do?" He touched my thigh.

"Nothing, I just need to feel this and deal with it. I can't keep running from my feelings." He draped his arm around my shoulder as he returned to his seat next to me and warmed my flesh. The smell of him, that deep husk of man. I couldn't resist it. I took a deep breath and leaned my head back as I continued to think about all that had happened. "What do you think she showed her?"

"I don't know," Rhys sighed. "Visions from the ancestors, well, they're rarely ever about picnics and roses."

"Yeah, that's what I was afraid of."

CHAPTER 23

"*You remember I said I would recruit more help?*" Maggie bounced into the room. As much as she tried to make us believe she was okay, the days that passed didn't work to convince me.

She'd successfully helped Roxanne remember the potion ingredients and the spell that was used to tie my mother's life to my father's. Unfortunately, she was so weak that Roxanne had to call some witches from the coven to help enact the spell. She'd been in her new hideout, her bedroom, most of the time. She said she was preparing for her role in the coming battle and resting as we had requested, but something felt odd about it.

"Yeah," the effort it took to pretend as if I wasn't worried about her was straining. It was bad enough, with all that she had been through, but it seemed like we just kept throwing more and more at her. The last thing she needed was my feeling sorry for her.

"Well, help has arrived!" She beamed as she pointed back to the door where three people had entered. Two familiar faces and one that I had never seen before.

"Oh, my god!" I gasped and jumped up to hug my friends, Latasha and Straught. I never thought I would see them again.

The last time I saw Straught, the tall, dashingly handsome bartender, he was behind a bar handing out drinks to girls who crushed on him but had no chance in hell of being with him. Trust me; it didn't stop them from trying. Drunk chicks will do anything in their power to get with a guy who looked like a superhero with green eyes and arms tattooed with bioluminescent ink.

Every time I saw him, he showed off his ink. Somehow, they always looked different. I used to question if they were real or airbrushed. It wasn't as if he could get fresh tattoos every day. Latasha was one of my closest friends before all hell broke loose.

She was the one who pushed me to step outside of my shell and often begged me to leave behind my rugged wear. That is exactly why it shocked me to see my short friend as she stood in front of me looking all bad ass in jeans, a leather jacket, and combat boots!

"What are you doing here?" I asked, but before anyone could answer, I turned to Maggie with follow-up questions. "Why are they here? They shouldn't be involved in any of this!"

"Explanation time guys, and quickly, please." Maggie urged them on, "preferably before I get my head chomped off!"

"Well, Sy, there is something you never learned about me." Straught spoke and smiled the same thousand-watt smile that made girls swoon. "I'm a vampire." He waved his hands and bowed as if awaiting applause.

"What?" My jaw damn near hit the floor. He didn't seem vampiric at all. No pale skin or blood sucking. Well, not that I ever saw. It did kind of explain the mystery tattoos on his arms. Could a vampire even get a permanent tattoo?

"Well, that is really a loose term when you think about it. I mean, there are so many kinds, but I would be your standard, run-of-the-mill, bite on the neck kind. And now," He turned to Latasha, "so is she."

"What?" I looked at Latasha, who smiled and then back to Straught. "What did you do? Why would you turn her?!" I was ready to fight, but Latasha held me back.

"Hold on, I was only helping!" He held his hands up in defense. "She was a complete mess after you left and she started going around asking questions and digging up thing she had no business knowing about. Those protectors of yours weren't the quietest clean-up crew."

"What?" I shook my head. "Clean-up crew?"

"The men lead by the mermen," He clarified. "They left behind a lot of evidence. Very sloppy. It wasn't hard for her to connect the dots. And of course, figure out that there was more to your leaving than just a sudden desire for relocation. I turned to her to protect her, and also to give her a bit of her sanity back. As a vampire, no one would try to mess with her, especially when aligned with my people. She also got to see the world for what it really was and not feel like she was losing her mind."

"Dammit, I'm so sorry." I looked at Latasha. "I didn't know you were going through so much. Leaving was supposed to keep you safe."

He had to give her back her sanity. What the hell had she gone through? All that time I thought leaving her behind would eliminate the drama of the supernatural world and let her resume a normal human life. Fuck if I wasn't completely wrong. I pulled her into my arms tighter than before.

"None of this is your fault, Sy. Girl. I'm just glad I got my own little lure now and I don't have to worry about picking up your leftovers!" She smiled and I could see her extended fangs. "Besides, being a vampire is badass, and that pesky aging thing is of no concern to me. I get to look fly forever!"

"Well, I guess I'm glad that you're okay. I hate that worrying about me put you through so much." It was so good to have her there alive and well, though, technically speaking, she was undead. Over her shoulder, the other new guest leaned against the wall as if she didn't want to be there at all. "What about her?"

"Oh. She isn't with us." Latasha shrugged and looked at Straught, who confirmed that the girl did not arrive with them.

"This is Menaria, also a vampire, of sorts." Maggie bounced over to the girl, laid her head on her shoulder, and smiled. She stared at her with loving eyes that gave me pause. What the hell was that about?

"Not your run-of-the-mill blood sucking type. I'm more like an alien, vampiric creature." The girl smiled, but somehow still seemed utterly uninvolved or worried about what was happening. True talent. She didn't acknowledge the puppy love looks she was getting from Maggie.

She played with a small orb that hung from a chain around her neck. It looked similar to the one around my neck, and the chain looked familiar as well. Unlike my stone, her orb glowed. She noticed the attention I was giving to it and tucked it away protectively into her jacket.

Menaria wore similar attire to Latasha. Jeans, a dark top, and leather jacket, but she wore Adidas instead of combat boots and the shirt under her jacket wasn't as form fitting. My guess was that vampires had no real perception of the temperature. While the rest of us dabbed sweat from our brows, they looked completely unbothered by the sticky heat.

"Menaria is my friend." Maggie chimed in and smiled at the impassive vampire again. "We met a while ago when I was on a trip to Chicago. I was actually there to do recon on the new siren that had everyone up in arms. This was long before you found out who you were. Menaria had a minor problem of her own and I helped her out. Now she is here to return the favor."

"One demon after another might as well keep up the trend." Again, Menaria shrugged off the situation and stared at the ceiling. What was this girl's problem?

"Well, thank you, Menaria, for coming to help us." I extended my hand to her, which she shook and smiled just enough to relay that she was on our side, but not enough to make her seem in any way concerned with what was actually happening. The girl had skill! I didn't know whether I should hug her or show her the door.

"There are others coming as well." Demetrius spoke. He had been absent since Malachi left. He and Verena held up together, confirming their bond, no doubt.

"Who?" I asked as Verena's head appeared over his shoulder.

I had the feeling the two of us needed to talk. The

topic of that conversation I wasn't sure about, but I knew she would be useless to us if she were holding on to any mixed or hurt feelings. Her guilty expression meant there was something she needed to work through. The woman got her man. She should be happy!

"Well, hello there, little siren." Cecile spoke from the open doorway. Fireflies flew in a halo around her head, making her look like an angel.

The last time I saw the woman, she was working her magic in the small shack, floating in the middle of the swamp. It was my first visit to New Orleans with the Denali brothers. She spun her magic to tell me what she saw in my future. The news was neither comforting nor inspiring. It also felt as if she knew exactly where my relationship with the brothers was headed. Disaster.

"Where are my boys?" She opened her arms as if they were already waiting to hug her.

"Cecile, it's so good to see you. I'm so glad that you could make it." Though I welcomed her, the witch looked past me.

She barely smiled in my direction. I never knew what I had done to upset her, but she was the same the first time we met. She only helped me because the brothers asked her to. I guess seeing how I would eventually hurt them made me a hard person for her to like.

She looked the same, as if she hadn't changed her clothing in all the time it'd been since I'd first seen her. Faded jeans and a loose fitted tie dye shirt hung from her shoulders. Bangles and dangles, she was adorned in jewelry that made her look like what most would a psychic to look like.

"Well, it wasn't as if it was a long journey. My home is just a little ways from here. Demetrius, baby," she headed over to the eldest brother and pinched his cheek like he was a child. "Where is your brother?"

As if summoned, Malachi appeared, though we thought he'd moved far away from the house. I wondered when he'd come back and if his brother had called him.

"Cecile? What are you doing here?" He crossed the room to embrace the woman.

My heart stopped for a moment. I hadn't seen him since he'd walked away from me the night after I'd chosen Rhys to take Demetrius' place as my bonded mate. I wanted to ask so much of him. We needed to talk, but his body language told me he wasn't there for me. He kept his back at an odd angle, turned just enough so he couldn't see me.

"I'm here to help, of course. This is the way things were supposed to happen. Whatever happens, you remember that." She touched his face and this time the sorrow was lighter, still there, but it didn't weigh as much. It had been there every time she laid eyes on the man. What was it she saw? What was it she envisioned for him? She looked over to Menaria. "Interesting girl, interesting power. You will do well."

"Talk about cryptic." Menaria rolled her eyes. "Where can I snooze?" She fussed and Maggie led the way to her own room, which they would share. My brow raised as I watched them leave together. Something was there. I didn't want to speculate, but it was damned hard not to.

"Cecile." Demetrius spoke as he wrapped his arms around the seer and hugged her tightly.

"My boy, I know there is much for us to discuss. I'm glad that you are here." She kissed his cheek, and something over his shoulder caught her eye. She eyed the bare space around Malachi's neck. Moving away from his brother, she walked over and laid her hand where his medallion usually lay. "You have strayed." She watched his face closely again with saddened eyes.

"Not far," he smiled reassuringly, but Cecile was clearly not convinced. Grayed eyebrows furrowed at him and her wrinkled face frowned.

"Far enough. Where can we go? We need to be alone." She asked me, but I didn't know the answer to her question.

"I-" Where would he be comfortable? As far as I knew, he didn't even want to be in the house to begin with. It was still a shock to see my brooding ex-friend standing there. I didn't even know if I could call him a friend anymore.

"I have a place." Malachi spoke, still positioned so he could not see me..

"Fine, fine, I will go with you. Little siren," she laid a motherly hand on his face before she turned to me again. "I will return to you later."

All I could do was nod in agreement and watch as the pair left.

"Anyone else?" I asked, as Maggie bounced back into the room. If there were any more people who were going to shock the hell out of me, I would need to be prepared. She seemed just as surprised to see Malachi there, but just in case. Cecile still was no easy pill to swallow.

"No one that I've invited. We have the power of the coven along with the ancient blood line in Ebon. We need to strategize now, let everyone know what role to play."

"I've invited some friends, but they won't be here for a while." Demetrius admitted. "We will need all the help we can get."

"Yeah, you're right." I looked at Rhys. "Can you gather everyone we have here in the dining room? I need to take care of something first."

"Sure, are you okay?" Demetrius pulled me away from the group and Verena bristled.

"Yeah, just, once again, I need a moment to clear my head. It's a lot to take in and process all at once, but I'll be okay. I'm glad that you could find us so much help. Thank you."

"No problem, that's what I'm here for." He nodded and turned to leave the room. He grabbed Verena's hand as he moved to exit, but I wanted her to stay.

"Verena, can we talk?" I called out, and they both stopped.

"Um. Yes, of course." She let go of Demetrius' hand. He looked at her to make sure she would be okay. Both of them needed to chill out. It wasn't as if I was going to bite her ass.

"There are just a few things I would like to discuss with you; I thought we could catch up a bit." I smiled as I spoke and hoped it would add softness to my tone and ease their overdramatic worries.

"Oh?" Verena turned to me and finally Demetrius left the room, and allowed us to be alone.

"Yes, I figured now is a good a time as any to discuss our friendship, if it can be called that," I left the statement open ended for her to confirm or deny.

What did she think of me? Would she ever be able to see me as an actual friend? I didn't know where things were headed, but I hoped to keep in contact with Demetrius, even if Malachi chose not to. In order to do that, things had to be squashed between the two sirens in his life.

"I'd like to think that we are, or at least that we can be again." She smiled and leaned against the wall of the hallway. The foyer seemed so much bigger with everyone out of it.

"Good, well, our friendship has had its share of hiccups. I just wanted to be sure to take a moment to tell you how happy I am that you're with Demetrius. I'm happy to see him happy. You're the reason for that, so thank you."

"You're thanking me? Wow! I never thought I'd hear that coming from you. I mean, I thought you'd be upset with me, pissed off, or feel betrayed." She chuckled. "Guess I had you all wrong. But it sounds like a lot of people have been wrong about you."

"How many times have I tried to tell you?" I threw my hand up in the air and laughed. "No, but seriously. I'm thrilled for you two. There was no way I would have ever made Demetrius happy; my heart wasn't in it. Yours is, and I can see that. Besides, it means that I get to be with Rhys, which is what I really want."

"It's good you know that you have that. It seems

so daunting, even now, being connected to Demetrius, I'm overwhelmed, but I know it's good for me, it's good for him, and we balance each other." She fiddled with her fingers. This was a side of her she'd never shown before. Vulnerability and nerves. This was good for her. It softened her.

"Yeah, I get that."

"It sucks for Malachi, though." She frowned and looked at the door that he'd just exited with Celia.

"Yeah," My gaze followed hers. "It really does."

CHAPTER
24

Rhys was already getting everyone in order. Our crew had grown so much and it felt good to know that there were so many people on my side. We stuffed the small dining room to the rim with people, and Roxanne was at her happiest, feeding them all. Once everyone had a drink in his or her hand and a stacked plate, she settled in.

"Thank you all for coming. Rhys and I have been thinking about our situation and believe that we've come up with a solution to the problem." I addressed the room. "As you all know, my mother, Siliya, is tied to Alderic. A spell linked her life to his. Understandably, I have no interest in losing my mother through this. Ebon and Roxanne have figured out the spell to release her from this link, but I've asked them to hold off with reason."

"We think," Rhys took over, "that we can use their

bond to our advantage. As long as he thinks we cannot free her, Alderic won't have his guard up. He sees her as his an insurance plan. If we can keep that bond in place, and use that presumption in our favor, we can trap him, subdue him long enough for the spell to release Siliya, and then once she is free, we will take care of Alderic."

"Do you really think it will be that simple?" Demetrius retorted.

"Simple? No. No one here thinks this will be a simple task. Even with the narrow vulnerability allowed by his overconfidence, Alderic is a very worthy opponent. He has planned this for decades and has accounted for every moment, but this link was not in his plan. This is our opening, and we must take advantage of it."

"How long will we have to keep him subdued?" Menaria asked lazily from a chair closest to the exit. "How long will it take for you to break the link?"

"Five minutes is all that we will need." Ebon nodded at Menaria, who smiled and straightened her posture.

"This sounds really risky. Are you sure that you want to play it this way?" Verena asked. She understood how important keeping my mother alive was to me. She knew how affected I was by her absence before.

"That's because it is risky." I answered her question. "But I challenge any of you to come up with a plan that isn't."

I looked around the room at frowned up faces. No one had an answer because there wasn't an easy one. There was no path that led to us getting out unscathed. Alderic made sure of it.

"My mother knows the plan," I continued. "She is well aware of the uncertainty of it. The fact of the matter is; she is already in harm's way and if we eliminate the tie between the two of them, that may very well just put a direct target on her back. The moment they are free of one another, he will have no reason to keep her alive. Leaving her connected to him as long as possible also works to keep her safe."

"What about a sleeping spell or something? You said whatever happens to one happens to the other, right?" Demetrius asked, now trying to figure out how we would subdue my father.

"Yes, but that isn't a definite. Alderic was able to sustain himself even though Siliya was under a spell. I'm sure that this is something he would have thought out. Over the years, he would have, if nothing else, safeguarded himself from any attack of that nature."

"So how is this plan any different? If a spell won't work, what makes you think this will?"

"Because we won't be using magic. We will have to physically harm her, enough to subdue, but not enough to kill."

"Seriously? You want us to beat up your mom?" Latasha's eyes were wide with disbelief. "I don't know if I can do that."

"It's the only way." My mother stood in the doorway. She'd been sleeping for quite some time. I didn't want to wake her, but she should have been a part of the meeting. She needed her rest after all she had been through and because of all that was to come. "I've been through worse, and I've already taken my fair share of shots. What's a few more?"

"Who exactly is supposed to be the one to do this?" Demetrius asked. "I'm here for the cause, but I'm not hitting a woman."

"I will." Roxanne stepped forward. "It won't be easy, but I will."

"Okay, so, witch mama is going to pound on siren mama to subdue warlock daddy?" Menaria recapped. "Just want to make sure that I got everything clear."

"Yes, and once he is subdued, Ebon and Roxanne, with the help of the other witches, will work to remove the tie. When we have the all clear, I will use my power to overcome my father. We need everyone in on this. He won't come alone. He isn't that foolish or shortsighted."

"Do you think he has some other group of witches aligned with him?" Demetrius looked at Rhys for the answer, knowing that he had the closest insight into

Alderic's life.

"Possibly, though I never saw him interact with anyone, not that he would have allowed me to see a meeting like that. There are other supernatural beings out there that do not share the same disdain for him; we can't count them out of the equation at this point. He's helped a lot of people, a lot of them not the nicest of sorts. I doubt he'd do that without a promise of a return on the favor. What better time than right now to call and cash in on all of those IOUs?"

"You said there were others coming. Who are they?" If Alderic was going to have buddies with him, we needed more help. Demetrius called others, but would that be enough?

"You met them once before." Demetrius answered. "Our adopted family."

"Tylia?" I smiled around the name of the siren who taught me to shift.

I hadn't seen her since we had to flee from her home when the coven sent their lynch men out to get me. I could see the long mess of a doo she wore on her head that fell past her shoulders and made her short stature look that much smaller. She was the adopted mother of wayward mermen, werewolves, and other creatures. Those who were without family became her own. This included Malachi and Demetrius.

"Yes, she is bringing the entire crew. They should be here shortly." Demetrius' tone lightened as he thought of them.

Of course, he would be happy to have them coming. They were his family, after all. Being near the people you loved and cared for was its own sort of high. That understanding came back to me as I looked around the table at all the concerned faces. Even in that moment with hell on the horizon, it was good to be surrounded by people I loved.

"What else can we do?" Verena stood to refill Demetrius' plate with food, but shook her head because Roxanne had already grabbed him some more grub. She took the plate from Rhys' semi-overbearing mother and returned to her seat.

"We can prepare, practice our strategies, and wait. He is definitely bringing the fight to us." Rhys stood at the head of the table; it was time for him to dish out the heavy duty work.

"How can you be sure?" Menaria leaned on her elbows and pushed away the plate of food Roxanne had sat in front of her. Perhaps vampires didn't eat regular food.

"Alderic is a gamer at heart. Everything he does is a puzzle. Something to be solved." Rhys explained. "If he wanted us to come to him, he would have already started sending over clues and riddles for us to solve.

266

That isn't happening. The only actual message we have gotten came through Noreen. That was purely a message of his intent.

"He attacked Siliya here, which is another show of how he can reach us even if we can't reach him. It's the same with the dreams that Syrinada has been having. He is bringing the fight to us and we damn well better be prepared to take on whatever he has to throw at us."

"In that case, we better start training to defend ourselves against him." Demetrius had already finished half his plate when he stood, wiping the food from his mouth. "Rhys, you sound like you know the most about what we are up against. You're going to need to tell us what we should do. What should we be on the lookout for? What are his weak spots?"

"I can definitely do that," Rhys nodded in agreement with Demetrius' comment. "Though, as far as weak spots, Syrinada and Siliya are all we have. Siliya, for obvious reason, is the connection between them, and Syrinada, for emotional ones." Rhys turned to me.

"Emotional?" I asked because I found it hard to believe my father had any genuine emotions for anyone besides himself.

"He will never admit it, but it hurt him when you decided not to stay with him. And I don't believe it's only because you wouldn't help him with his master plan. Yes, he had a grand design, and you were an important part of that design. We all know that much. I believe he thought you were going to welcome him with open arms and never question his motives. You didn't do that. Despite everything else that has happened, you are his daughter, and you rejected him."

"Fine, then we use that against him." I wouldn't allow any remorse to creep into my mind.

Alderic may have felt bad about my deciding not to entertain his evil plans. It may have even hurt him that I didn't become the daughter he dreamed of for more reasons than his interrupted plans for taking out the coven. None of that mattered. He was a bad person, and as far as I was concerned, he deserved what was coming to him.

"How?" For someone who appeared to be so lacking in concern of our situation, Menaria was being quite vocal.

"Maybe Sy can pretend that she wants to give in to dear old daddy?" Maggie offered as she popped another piece of food into her mouth. She had refilled her plate twice already and was looking to be going back for a third time.

"I highly doubt that will work. Alderic will sense if she is lying about something like that." Roxanne spoke, "Evil knows evil. If she doesn't actually accept it into herself, he can tell."

"Fine, so make him believe that you have." Menaria spoke again.

"How am I supposed to do that?" She could seriously go back to being quiet. The path of the conversation was not one that I wanted to continue, and the next person to add to the conversation would prove exactly why I wanted the detour.

"Give into him. You'll need to let yourself go." Ebon spoke for the first time. "It is a risk, but it is likely the best way to get the distraction we will need."

"You want me to give in to his evil? Isn't that exactly the thing that you have all been trying to avoid?" It was ridiculous. The entire time I'd known about my powers, my abilities, I had been working to prove that I wasn't this evil being for people to fear, and there Ebon was, sitting across the table from me and telling me to become just that!

"We will stop him before he really affects you." She said confidently.

"And if you don't?" I looked around the table, knowing most of them were already on board with the plan. "What happens to me if you can't stop him?"

"Then you will be lost to us and we will all likely die. The thing is, you can't live your life like that. That kind of fear will ultimately destroy you." The ghost spoke and everyone else hushed. "You have friends and family here who will fight like hell to keep from losing you. You have Rhys, who is now bonded to you. Believe in that bond and remain open to it. That link, the power in that bond, will be what saves you."

No one spoke after Ebon spoke her mind. The idea simply settled across us in the room. I would have to become the thing everyone feared most of me.

I looked at Rhys. "What do you think about this?"

"I think it's a good plan." His jaw tightened like he wanted another way, but he nodded because he knew this was the right move. "It makes sense. It's risky though. I'm not sure I am ready to risk losing you like that. It's ultimately up to you. Whatever you decide to do, I will support you through it all."

"Dammit," I took a deep breath and looked around the room one more time. "How bad can it be, really?"

"You know, that's what people usually say in movies, right before everyone dies." Maggie added and earned a shocked look from everyone in the room. "What?"

CHAPTER
25

The field was familiar. I'd been there before. It was a hard place to forget. Hell, it took a fight with the Kraken to make it there. The same land that was laid out in front of me was the same that I saw at the start of the walk. It was the journey of tests that I had to pass in order to get my stone. This time, the illusion was not lost on me.

This time, I realized that nothing I saw was real. Off in the distance was a long line of trees, and just like déjà vu, there was the figure of a man standing beneath them. Though the scenario was familiar, it was different in very important ways, ways that told me that there was a purpose to my being there again.

The last time I was in the field, the feeling of the grass blades between my toes consumed me. This time, I felt anxious and hyperaware of my surroundings. Nothing about the field welcomed or soothed me as it did before. The air was brisk, and sharp bursts of wind cut through me, keeping my mind even more alert than it was before.

The sky was odd; the coloring was off, and the clouds moved in a strange darting fashion that made me think of anxious children. There was something else lurking in the peripherals, it was the signature of something dark, evil.

Just as it had happened before, a few steps forward took me across the extensive field and left me standing just feet away from him. He was different this time; he wasn't the same person who met me with kind eyes and an eagerness to love me. There was love there, but it was buried beneath hatred and disappointment. We stared at each other silently, waiting for the other to speak.

"Are you ready for what is coming?" Alderic stood before me, cloaked in a long jacket with only his interlocked hands visible in front of him.

My father was a gorgeous man, and I wished I could enjoy him. I wished that being near him didn't make me sick to my stomach, that his evil heart didn't paint the powerful lines of his jaw and his smooth skin such an ugly color.

"I'm prepared." I spoke calmly.

He did nothing for me to be upset or defensive. Not yet. This was a meeting; this was his warning.

"How can you be so sure?" He tilted his head just slightly enough to display his confidence. He didn't believe me.

"Does it really matter?" I shrugged. "Are you going to hold off until you believe I'm ready to face you?"

He shook his head no, then looked at the sky as he spoke. "I will not hold back just because you are my daughter."

"I never expected you to; you've never been the fatherly type." The wind picked up and pushed my hair into my face. His hand was there to remove the strands.

"How I wish you could see me for what I really am." He tucked the hair behind my ear and returned to his previous position. Hands interlocked, and head tilted toward the sky. "I'm coming, and I will get what I want."

"Well, there is no need for this discussion then, is there?" I turned away from him, prepared to walk out of the dream world he'd conjured.

"Syrinada," he said my name.

I didn't want to stop, but I did. "What?"

"I do not take pleasure in hurting you." he announced with the same emotionless tone as always.

If I'd been a fool, I would have believed the

sentiment in his words. It would have made me happy to know that on some level, he cared. But I'd seen what he was capable of and knew that there was so much more behind his mask.

"Funny, your actions would do good to prove otherwise." I rejected his statement as the wind picked up again.

"This is beyond you." His voice had more force when he spoke. "This is greater than all of us."

"Whatever it takes to keep you getting up in the morning." I shrugged and continued walking away.

"I will only tolerate your insolence for so long!" He yelled after me.

I kept walking. I put one foot in front of the other and never looked back. Alderic didn't call out to me again. He didn't chase me. He simply let me go. Even though the space extended between us, I could still feel him as if he was standing right beside me. The touch of his power, the evil that had taken over his soul. This is what they expected me to take into myself. This is what they expected me to survive.

I awoke from a dream of the devil wrapped inside the arms of an angel. Rhys slept peacefully by my side and held me close to him. I wondered why life was so complicated. Why couldn't those sweat moments, waking up in the arms of the man I loved, be all there was? Why did it have to always be so much more drama and pain?

The sun peeked through the curtains of the window, and I could already smell the aromas coming from Roxanne's kitchen. If I didn't leave her home soon, I would have to join a weight loss program. As it was, I avoided the scale that sat on the bathroom floor like the plague! Still, my stomach growled.

"When in Rome!" I whispered before figuring out how to get away from the sleeping man at my side.

I didn't want to wake him, but slipping out of Rhys' hold wasn't easy. It took several wiggles, three shimmies, and a twist with a cat like landing to free myself without waking him. Quietly, I threw on a pair of sweats and a loose fitted tank top and slipped out the door.

The house was littered with bodies. It looked like more of Maggie's friends had arrived and taken over whatever space they could claim to rest. Some bodies looked familiar, but it was hard to tell who they were because of arms thrown across their faces or the pillows that hid them. I tiptoed through the halls, attempting not to wake any of them; some of them had clearly arrived after I'd gone to bed last night.

As expected, Roxanne was busy in the kitchen. Pots and pans were on the stove. The aroma of beignets came from the oven where she put them to keep them warm, and my stomach growled. As if she knew I was coming, she handed me a small bowl of fruits to snack on. After I took two bites, she ushered me to the counter, pointed to the chair, and handed a bowl of potatoes and a peeler. I went to work without question, popping fruit in my mouth between slices.

"Syrinada, it is good to see you again."

I turned my head to find a familiar face. Tylia was Demetrius and Malachi's adopted mother. She was short and stocky and the first time I met her, I thought she would kill me. She smiled at me behind the wild locks of her hair and held her arms out for an expected hug. I got up, eager to embrace the siren who showed me how to unleash my tail.

Painful as that first shift turned out to be, she was my tutor, and I could never repay her for all that she'd taught me in such a short time. Tylia was the only siren I knew that had succeeded in the Naiads Walk and earned her siren's stone. She didn't let the power go to her head. In fact, she led a simple life and gave me hope the same was possible for me.

"Tylia, I'm so glad that you came! Are the others with you? Are you all okay?" I rambled on while I tried to keep the juice from the strawberries in my mouth.

"Yes, the boys are all here," she looked over her shoulder. "I assume they are somewhere in that pile of limbs. We're all fine. I know the last time we saw one another, there were witches out to get us, but once they realized you weren't with us, and that I am far more powerful than the average siren, they backed off."

"I'm glad you're here." I hugged her again. "Demetrius told us he called you."

"Yes, he did, and he was quite adamant that we come and help, though it wasn't as if we were going to say no!" she smiled. "Now, Roxanne, for the tenth time, please let me help you cook!"

"Tylia, we have this conversation every time you come here!" Roxanne popped the back of Tylia's hand as she reached for a potato to peel. "You are not touching a thing in my kitchen!"

"You really need to let go of your control issues, woman." Tylia rubbed her hand and Roxanne rolled her neck and stuck her tongue out at the siren.

"You two know each other?" They interacted with each other like two old friends.

"Oh, yes, for ages now! And she is still just as stubborn as always." Tylia said and scowled at Roxanne.

"I am not stubborn; I am a proper hostess!" Roxanne defended herself and straightened the apron around her waist. "You don't see me barging into your kitchen when I visit you!"

"Right, because you have no manners!" Tylia laughed. "Anyone knows that once you've been to a person's house more than twice, you are no longer a guest. You are family, and family offers to help cook!"

"The potatoes are done." I slid the bowl over to Roxanne and picked up the bowl that she'd apparently refilled with fruit. I didn't see her do it, but she would never hear me complain about it.

"Thank you, Sy." Rhys' mother rolled her eyes at me as if she knew exactly what was about to come out of Tylia's mouth.

"Oh, so she can peel potatoes and yet I get scolded if I even dare to look at your water boiling?" Tylia frowned and threw her hands on her hips. "Okay, I see what this is! That's ageism!"

The two burst into laughter and I took that as my cue to leave. I snuck out of the door with my bowl in hand. I could finish my fruit in bed.

On the way back up to my room, I recognized each of the guys. Eric, the short funny one with light colored hair that complimented the lighter tones of his skin. Shelly was the tall one with dark brown skin, and a fro that made his head look three times its size. Charles was there as well. He was the brawn, muscular one, but shorter than me.

Three mermen, all alphas in their own right. Thank goodness that I already had a mate!

"Mmm, you brought me food? That's so sexy." My

mate, my man, was standing by the window, peering out into the world. He turned to me and smiled as I slowly pushed the door shut behind me.

"Umm, yeah, I sure did." I grinned around the strawberry I had just popped into my mouth.

"You are such a liar." Rhys laughed and pulled me into his arms.

"We have extra guests down there."

"Full house now." He kissed my neck and my knees buckled. Damn.

"Do you think it will be enough?" I asked, and he frowned.

I knew what he wanted, hell I wanted it to, but it was important to keep my mind clear. Besides, with so many extra ears in the house, it would be uncomfortable to get anything started.

"I think we have a good chance of succeeding in this." He tightened his hold on me.

"Rhys,"

"Yes?" he answered and picked a berry from the bowl I still held.

"I'm worried about taking his power into me, about what it will do to me." I searched his eyes for something to tell me how he truly felt. Was he just as worried?

"Sy, I am here, I will be here, and as long as this bond exists between us, there is nothing anyone can do to make me stop fighting for you." He took the bowl from my hands and placed it on the table. "You are mine and I will have you, no matter what I have to do to make sure that happens."

And just like that, I forgot about keeping my head clear. Dammit if I din't want them to hear us. A promise like that deserved a roll between the sheets.

CHAPTER 26

R *hys spent the next few days training* and preparing the assembled teams. He revealed all that he could about Alderic. His insight was the most valuable tool in our arsenal, and he reminded everyone to beware that Alderic was someone who easily adapted to change.

The knowledge he had, although it would help us prepare, was not to be taken as a rule. He told of the tricks he liked to play, the mind games, and sensory deceptions. Alderic had many surprise cards hidden up his sleeves and Rhys didn't even pretend to know them all.

We agreed Alderic wasn't alone. He wanted us to believe that he was, but I could sense it, and so could Rhys and Ebon. There was something dirty in the air. Something unfamiliar and it left traces of evil on everything it touched. There was more than just the magic he worked to play tricks on our minds. He was one step ahead of us, he always had been.

It was too bad we didn't have time to figure out who was helping him. On the fourth day, Alderic set off a bomb.

The house trembled, and the floorboards buckled and shifted. Where did it come from? There was no evidence of fire, no sign of ignition, but loud booms rang out and each time the walls shook more. Everyone scrambled to their feet, trying to find safety and protection from chunks of ceiling that fell from above.

"We have to get out of here!" Demetrius yelled out before he grabbed Verena and pushed her towards the door. "If we stay in here, the ceiling is going to come down on our heads!"

We all fled through whatever opening we could. People jumped out windows and pushed through the doors. We had to get free. Demetrius was right. If Alderic wanted to, he could have just brought the house down on our heads and been done with it, but I knew killing us wasn't the end game. He wanted to flush us out, and he had accomplished that.

Roxanne and my mother ran out ahead of me. Rhys was behind me. I tried to be sure everyone was free, but it was impossible to tell. Screams of pain told us that some had not made it out alive, or at least not without injury.

"To the trees!" Malachi yelled out.

Everyone bolted through the field into the wooded lands behind Roxanne's home. The night sky hid the dangers that waited for us, the demons that he had unleashed. As we hit the tree line, monsters emerged from the shadows. They snatched up two small witches. I watched in complete horror as the creatures pulled their limbs from their bodies and swallowed them behind rows of sharp teeth.

"Stop!" I screamed. "Stay out of the shadows!"

"We can't stay here. We're too exposed!" Malachi yelled back.

"I know we need to figure something out, but going in there is not the way." I looked around the group and counted who I could find.

"What the hell are those things?" Maggie caught up to me with Menaria on her heels.

"Demons." Malachi took a deep breath. "I can tell by the way they smell. Definitely demons."

"Demons?" Menaria smiled hungrily. "My kind of treat!" Without another word, she took off and darted into the trees.

"What the hell is wrong with that girl?" Verena caught her breath as she stopped running. "Does she have a damn death wish?"

"No, but she is hungry." Maggie smiled and pointed to the average sized girl standing at the trees. "Remember, she's not like the other vampires."

Though chaos continued around us, I couldn't take my eyes off Menaria. She reached the edge of the shadows, looked back at Maggie, and winked. A moment later, her jaw unhinged and her mouth opened so wide it looked like she would swallow her own head.

The features of her face changed to something sinister. Menaria took in a deep pull of air and, with that air, the dark souls of demons. They screamed, tried to pull away from her, and clawed at the ground, lifting chunks of earth, but nothing helped their effort. In a matter of minutes, Menaria swallowed three of them whole. She stood, features back to normal, waved to us, and took off deeper into the woods.

"Well, that was interesting." Latasha fell from the sky in front of us. "Don't look at me for any freaky shit like that!" She looked out into the trees. "Straught is out there with a few of our friends. Demons aren't an easy kill, but we can take them on a lot better than mortals can. We will do what we can to try to hold them at bay."

"Be careful, please." I pulled her into a hug. "I just got you back. Don't want to lose you again."

"You too, Sy." She hugged me tightly and took off back into the trees.

"The vampires will take the demons out from the back side; we can hold them off on our end." Malachi spoke up and slapped his brother on the shoulder. "Let's go!"

With little to no effort, unlike I had ever seen him turn before, Malachi called to the blood of his father and the demon that dwelled within him pulled to the surface. His body stretched another foot taller than his normal 6 foot height, and his arms bulged with veins. His skin became discolored and his face distorted. Malachi didn't wait for his brother to join him. He took off running into the night, and within seconds, I could hear his fight.

"I'll be back for you." Demetrius pulled Verena into his arms, removed the medallion from around his neck, and handed it to her. "Keep this safe for me." He still needed it to keep his monster at bay and that charm was the only thing that did.

He kissed the tips of his fingers and pressed it against her stomach. Maggie and I shared a questioning look. As his demonic side came to the surface and his dreads became thick locks of flame, he followed the path of his brother.

Verena looked at me with sad eyes.

"He'll be back." I tried to reassure her, but even I was worried, especially after his insinuating gesture.

"I hope so." She nodded.

~*~

A loud groaning sound accompanied the trembles of the ground. Just ahead, between the demon-infested tree line and our group, the field split, and two large pillars emerged. Strange text that was carved into the stone glowed red hot. Between the pillars were two doors. They looked heavy and ancient and were covered in blood.

Smeared across the old stone, made by the hands of the damned, were crimson colored markings of death. My heart felt heavy, and I struggled to breathe as I watched the doorway emerge.

"What the hell is that?" Maggie asked, and even though I'd never seen it before, something inside me knew exactly what we were looking at.

"The gates," Ebon was there to answer Maggie's question.

"Gates?" Maggie looked at Ebon, who had Roxanne by her side. "Gates to where?"

"To the afterlife." Roxanne stepped forward and grabbed my mother's hand.

"Not just the afterlife, those are the dark gates." Ebon turned to me. "He is starting the ritual to get to your grandfather."

"You're telling me he is opening up the doorways to hell? My grandfather is in hell?" That was the answer that sat in the pit of my stomach. The one that pure intuition provided me with long before she ever spoke the truth into existence.

How else would Alderic's magic be so dark and so vicious? Where else would he be pulling that type of evil from, if not from hell?

"That's exactly what he is doing." Ebon stepped forward, holding her hands out towards the gates. "Your grandfather was the one of the darkest warlocks this world ever knew. He had one foot in the underworld long before we relieved this world of his presence. Your father wants that power. He wants to use your grandfather's magic to bring the evil that lives on that other side into our world."

"How is this happening here?" I looked around to the shadows that appeared to be moving. "Why here?"

"This land has gone through so much. We'll never know how blood was spilled on these grounds. Your grandfather caused a lot of that. He pinpointed this place long ago, and he wasn't the only one who tried bringing about this evil, but he was sure as hell the one to come closest to succeeding." Ebon continued her explanation as the others regrouped.

With the ground split, those on our side of the crack were safe from the demons. I counted the heads around me again, this time noting that there were three fewer than before. The men Demetrius called had arrived just before things went to hell, so I wasn't sure how many people I should have a count of.

"We stopped him and so many others." Ebon kept her eyes on the gateway. "Hurricane Katrina, it wasn't just a natural disaster, it was another attempt to bring about the end of times. We stopped evil then, like so many other times before, and we must again today! It has always been our duty to stop that from happening, to protect this world from what lies on the other side of that threshold. Now it is your responsibility as well."

"If he succeeds?" I asked because I needed to know. What would happen if we couldn't stop my father from getting what he wanted?

"He must not; you must not let that happen." Ebon was stern in her words. It was all in her eyes. The unspoken warning of what horrors would follow if we failed. I saw it. Death, destruction, and an evil like nothing I would ever know. She had witnessed it firsthand.

"We cannot let that happen!" I turned to the group.

"He has already accessed that plane. That is why those demons are here. If he opens that door, there's no way we're going to survive!" Rhys spoke above the sounds of demonic cries.

"Alderic!" I screamed out into the night. "Show yourself!"

"Ah, dear daughter, finally, you called?" Alderic appeared, the same as he was in the field, cloaked in black, hands locked in front of him, but this time he smiled.

"Stop this!" I yelled at him and he laughed at my anger.

"Why should I? I am so close to victory." The skies behind his head, already dark from night, grew darker. The light of the stars and the moon dimmed as a curtain of obscurity pulled across the sky.

"You can't do this, not without me." I knew what the plan was, but with literal gates to hell sitting just a few feet from where we stood, there was no way I could draw that evil into me.

I hoped Roxanne and Ebon could free my mother from him before I did what had to be done.

"Well, the thing about that is, you aren't the only one capable of being the vessel I need." Again, he smiled. His eyes raised, checkmate.

"You cannot have my mother!" I looked back to where she stood with the others. If he thought I'd trade my life for hers, he had a lot more to learn about his daughter.

"Oh, you sirens are all so vain! Did you think for a moment that I would rely solely on you? Did you think I would not have a backup? Once my backstabbing buddy cast the spell that kept your mother alive, I came up with a new plan, an alternative. A new vessel."

"What the hell are you talking about?" I looked back at Roxanne, who shrugged.

"Syrinada," He paused and stepped to the side. Behind him, a tall girl stood. Though she was clearly younger than I was, the features of her face showed she was not innocent. Smooth honey skin and an afro that stood high on her head. She stood with a blank face, eyes dark as night. "I'd like you to meet your sister, Imara."

"Sister?" I looked back to my mother, who had remained close to Roxanne. She shook her head, confirming she didn't know who the girl was.

"Yes, it would turn out that there are other powers, powers that aligned so much better with what I was trying to do here. Your sister, my darling Imara, is like you in some ways, but in others, she is oh, so different."

"What the hell are you talking about?"

"Imara here, beautiful as she is, is a succubus. You know of them, yes, demons who feed off sex. I trapped her mother long enough to produce this beautiful girl. As long as I possess this," He held up a small stone. "She is mine to control, with none of that self-conscious bullshit that comes with you! Imara is the vessel; she is the key!"

"I will not let you do this!" I yelled. "You cannot open the gates of hell just because you miss your damn daddy."

"Haven't you figured it out? It's not me you have to worry about." He blew on the stone and as it glowed red, so did Imara's eyes.

She said nothing, made not a single sound or warning before she launched at me. I dove out of the way and she fell to the ground, but was right back up to her feet, ready to pounce again. Her teeth bared and her skin shifted into a sickly color.

"Stop this! You don't want to do this!" I yelled at her, but it was useless. She was Alderic's puppet and nothing I said would get through to her. Hell, I didn't even know if she was evil or not, but something inside of me couldn't fathom the idea of hurting her.

I tried to dodge the next launch of attacks, but she fell right on top of me. Her grip was firm and her body felt as though it weighed ten times what I would have expected. Her face was stone, motionless as she leaned into me. Unable to move, I struggled, but she kept me pinned in place.

She leaned forward, lowering her face to mine, then pressed her lips against mine. At first I was disgusted, then I was terrified as I felt the life leaving me. Red and gold strands pulled from my mouth into hers.

"No!" Rhys screamed out before a burst of air sent my newly introduced sister flying off of my body and into the tree just beside us. She fell like a log and hit the ground, but within moments was charging at me again.

"Stop!" I yelled as I struggled to get up, but still she came. Rhys hit her again, and she flew back, stunned for just a moment longer, but it wouldn't keep her down.

"Alderic! Syrinada, take him out." Rhys threw another blow at the girl and looked over his shoulder at my father, who laughed. "I got her. Take care of him!"

I turned to Alderic. In my efforts to protect myself from my sister, I hadn't noticed the havoc he was causing. The screams of my friends and family rang out as the pillars glowed. "Can you keep her at bay?"

"Not for long." He pushed another powerful blow at her.

"I can help." Maggie held her side, and there was blood on her fingers. She had been hurt, and badly.

"Maggie!' I put my hand up to heal her.

"Sy, not now. You need your strength. Stop Alderic!" She pushed my hand away. "Roxanne and Ebon are going to work the spell now. The old plan is out the window."

"Wait," I hesitated, but there wasn't time for that. Everyone around me fought like hell to stop my father. I had to do more.

"Syrinada, go!" Rhys yelled at me again.

CHAPTER
27

I ran away from Rhys and Maggie, who threw everything they had at Imara. Still, she fought to get past them to me. Alderic gave her one goal: take me out, and she was determined to make him proud.

A line of witches and Mermen stood as a border around my mother, where Ebon and Roxanne worked to reverse the magic that tied her to Alderic. He pummeled the wall of bodies with repeated hits, trying to break the line, but their collected magic stood strong against his.

Celia and Tylia stood at the head of the group. Hands clasped together, they faced Alderic head on. He concentrated his power on them. They were the strongest in the group. If he could take them down, the others would quickly crumble. They held their own, but their magic was weakening. He was stronger than we thought, and with the demonic doors that sat waiting to be opened, his powers were growing.

A sharp bolt of red hot magic shot out and struck the barrier the two had erected. It left behind a crack in their shield. I had to help, and fast. Just across the field, I saw Malachi emerge, a demonic presence fueled by the fight. He ran for Alderic. I turned and bolted for Celia and Tylia. If I could combine my power with theirs, I could stop him from penetrating the protection before they set my mother free.

We were both too late. Another shot of magic hit them just as Malachi crashed into Alderic and knocked him to the ground. The blaze lit up the field. The barrier exploded, shattering like glass and sent the collective of witches flying to the ground.

"Celia!" Malachi cried out. He jumped to his feet, leaving his fight with Alderic to run to her side. It was too late; she was gone. He pulled her into his arms and held her. His tears, visible drops of red against grayed flesh.

Mourning the loss of the woman closest to him, Malachi left himself vulnerable. Alderic stood to his feet and held out his hand to Malachi's back.

"No!" I screamed out and my fear for my friend pushed my power to the brink.

The earth rumbled with my anger, and Alderic turned to me. I held out my arms to him and called for the power that filled his body, the power that tied him to my grandfather and to the evil that dwelled on the other side of the doors he was so desperately trying to open. I pulled it from him. All that I could. Wave after wave of darkness crashed into me. It nearly forced me over, but I held my ground.

Alderic was strong, he wouldn't give up without a fight. He pushed back, tried to stop me from taking away the power that belonged to him. I continued to draw in the energy and the pull expanded until I felt the life of everything and everyone around me coming into my body. His power, his stolen magic, was different from anything I'd had before.

The power that came from Alderic and his demonic forces was heavy and made me feel sick. What came from the others, the witches, and the mermen, who all fell to the ground as they suffocated beneath the strength of my will, was what felt so intoxicating, so alluring.

Ebon and Roxanne were the only ones who could hold against me. They protected my mother and continued to do their magic. They had to complete the spell. As I got stronger, Ebon called for help and the spirits I'd met once before appeared to form a circle around them. Their hands locked and their eyes glowed with the light of the afterlife.

Imara, unaffected by my power, tried again to attack me. I could feel her sinister magic approaching from behind. It was Malachi who jumped to his feet and bolted for her. The impact of their bodies as they crashed to the ground was barely audible over the sounds of the life that was pulling into me.

The trees withered and the blades of grass that covered the ground all turned dry. I couldn't hold it much longer. My thoughts grew darker as the evil overwhelmed the good. It felt so satisfying. The power and the strength made me laugh as I watched my father quiver and fall to his knees. Alderic was nothing, just a man, a man hungry for power and that power was mine!

The skies lit up. An electric show of lightning broke through the dark blanket and struck the ground. Time and time again, the strikes rang out. Each burst of energy fed into my strength, and I reveled in it.

"Syrinada, please stay with me." The voice in my mind was calm. He always remained cool under pressure, even when the world was going to hell.

"Rhys?" I called back to him, my eyes darting around to find his face, but I couldn't.

"I can feel you, the strength, the power, the darkness, don't give into it. Stay with me." He pleaded with me softly. He loved me and he wanted me. "Stay with me."

"It feels so good. Just feel it, Rhys. The power, I just…"

"Don't give into it, please. Think of your mother, think of me, of the life we want to have together." There was pain in his voice. "None of that will be possible if you lose yourself now."

"I don't want to lose you, Rhys."

"And you never will, Syrinada; I am here. Just hold on to me." His voice echoed inside my head. I had to hold on.

"Hurry!" I screamed out to Roxanne and Ebon while I still held on to some of the clarity Rhys brought back to me. Alderic was still fighting, but I'd weakened him, but it wouldn't last long. If I wanted to, I could take him out, but I had to make sure it was safe for my mother.

The dark magic was returning to him. Though he couldn't pull it back from me, he could call more from the other side of the gate. I felt it grow darker as it entered his back and exited his chest, cyphering into my body.

"It's done!" Ebon called out. "Finish it!"

"I can't. The door, the magic is coming through!" Ebon left the safety of the barrier to come to me. "No, don't!"

"Use my power, Syrinada. Use it to fight!" She spread her arms and fell to her knees, and offered her power to me."

"Are you sure?" I looked down at her then back at my father. "I don't want to hurt you."

"I'm already dead! Do it!"

I turned my right hand to her and pulled in her energy. It balanced my father's with clean light that felt like a fresh shower for my brain. Tainted thoughts fled my mind completely and without the haze of evil, everything was clear to me. Rhys was down, injured, but alive. Malachi still struggled with Imara, who stared at me with hatred. Each time she launched herself at me, his demonic form crashed into her and prevented her from approaching.

Demetrius was kneeling at the tree line, holding a limp Verena in his arms. He cried out in pain and I had to turn away. Bodies were everywhere. Witch and vampire and mermen, and in front of me, my father. Alderic. He clutched the earth around him and called to the other side, the darkest side, Hell.

The doors to the gateway shook, the ground trembled, and the squeak of the hinges, long since locked in place, called out. He was getting his wish. Imara stopped moving. She stood up and held her hands to the door. Her eyes closed and her head tilted back. It was happening. Alderic smiled and laughed.

"You are no match for me!" He yelled out above the endless noise. "He is coming and there is nothing you can do about it!"

"You will not do this!" I called back.

"There is nothing you can do to stop me!" Alderic struggled to stand but kept his bravado. "I'm too strong and once he is here, there will be no one strong enough to face his power!"

"Well, he isn't here yet!" I stepped forward. "I say I just take you out now and we can be done with all this."

"You kill me and you kill your pathetic mother!" He laughed. "Or did you forget the magic that connects us? Her life is mine. We are one!"

"That's where you're wrong." I pointed to my mother, who stood strong behind me, unaffected as he was. "Or did you not feel that bond break? It's done, and so are you."

"What? That's impossible, I still feel her!" He screamed out, but I looked to Roxanne, who nodded. It was done.

Ebon was still on her knees, vulnerable to attack. The gates shook with the threat that waited on the other side. Alderic claimed to still feel the connection to my mother, but I had no choice but to act. Roxanne and Ebon had confirmed that their spell worked, and I knew neither of them would lie about it. I had to trust in them. Alderic would do anything to distract me long enough for those gates to open.

The doors groaned again and shook, and there was no more time for second guessing. With the strength of

Ebon combined with my own, I focused on my father. Just as I coaxed the life back into the plants that had all but lost it, I pulled it from within his body. The cloak he wore burned away to reveal a bruised man. The power that ripped from him left cuts along his flesh.

Each time I pulled more, a fresh wound opened, and he cried out. Layer after layer until the darkness was gone, and all that was left was man. Sad, confused, lonely, and heartbroken — that was the core of my father. He was a man who had lost it all and then lost his way.

Before I snuffed the final ember of his life out, I felt it. Love, love for me and for Imara, love for his father. That moment was the hardest, realizing what he was really capable of and still having to continue to take that from him.

"Goodbye." I whispered as his eyes locked onto mine. A solitary tear fell down his cheek and watched in horror as his own daughter took his life away.

~*~

The world came back into focus, and Rhys' had his arms wrapped around me. I could breathe again after the pressure lifted from my chest. The demonic cries had stopped and the pillars, though still there, no longer glowed. The sounds and evil that I felt coming from the other side had ceased. My collected power eased away from me and returned to its rightful home within the trees, the land, and the people who surrounded me.

"Is it over?" I asked Rhys. The moon and stars had returned to the sky and their light lit his face.

"Yes, you did it." He smiled and kissed my forehead.

"Really? It's over?" I asked again because it felt too good to be true.

"Yes, it is." He laughed softly, pulled me into his arms and held me. I sobbed into his shoulder. It was over. Alderic was gone, and the pain could end.

Back on my feet, I took in all that happened. Demetrius still sobbed over Verena's body. He cried out and kissed her face. She was gone. Tylia prayed over the fallen Celia, and her adopted sons joined her in lifting the small witch from the ground to carry her body away from the carnage. I watched as people pulled themselves together and as they mourned for those who would never walk away from the battleground.

Menaria stood over Maggie's body, and I waited for the spunky girl to stand again. She would hop up from her place and start making funny remarks about how we had defeated the beast. She didn't move. It came together, slowly and painfully. Her chest did not move with the rise and falls of breaths. Her skin was pale, lifeless, and covered in blood.

"Maggie!" I ran away from Rhys and fell to my knees beside her. The same injuries that covered Alderic covered her. The wounds opened on her arms, legs and torso, where the dark magic left his body to return to the otherworld. She had the same marks! "How is this possible? What happened to her?!"

"Syrinada," Roxanne spoke and tried to pull me into her arms.

"What did you do?!" I screamed at the woman and pushed her away. "He said he could feel her. He said the connection was still there. It wasn't my mother, was it? Was it? You should have told me!"

"We couldn't remove it, we had to transfer it. Maggie was the one it had to be, his magic was already tied to her." Roxanne tried again to put her arm around me, but again I pushed her away and sobbed over the body of my friend.

"You sacrificed her!" I felt disgusted by their decision and betrayed by their omission. "There had to be another way! How could you do this? How could you let her die? She didn't deserve this!"

"This is the way it had to be." Ebon spoke softly to me. "Alderic's magic was present in her blood; it was her or you."

"You knew this would happen? You knew what would happen all along! Why didn't you tell us?" I pointed at the ghost. "Why didn't you give us a chance to stop this? She didn't have to die!"

"That was always her path, Syrinada." Ebon offered the only explanation she could. "She knew that and she accepted it."

"You can't believe that."

"We all must make tough choices, ones that are so hard to face. Trust me; no one knows this better than I." It didn't seem possible of someone who was a ghost, but tears fell down the small face of the girl. That is what she was; being centuries old didn't mean a damn thing. Ebon was a girl, forever frozen that way.

"Why didn't you tell me?" I looked at Roxanne and back to Ebon. "I just don't understand why you wouldn't let me know about this. How could you let this happen?"

"Maggie understood what was going to happen here. That's all that should matter now." Roxanne offered, as if knowing that someone I cared about willingly sacrificed herself for me was any better. Yes, I wanted my mother to live, but not at the expense of someone else.

"This is what you showed her! Isn't it?" I turned on Ebon and pulled away from my mother's hold.

"All that I can offer you is the truth. Maggie is a lot like me." Ebon nodded her head. "We were meant for something greater, to accept that purpose; to come to terms with what must be is what we both had to do. I gave myself for the greater good, and so did she."

I fell to my knees and pulled her close to my chest. Ebon's truth wasn't good enough. Nothing would ever be good enough. My friend was gone and there was nothing I could do to fix it. As hard as I reached with my magic, as strongly as I called for the life within her to return, there was nothing. She was gone. Still, I whispered in her ear, "Maggie, please come back to me, please."

THE END....

THE STORY CONTINUES...

THE SIREN SERIES

SiRen's Capture

USA TODAY BESTSELLING AUTHOR
JESSICA CAGE

4

ABOUT THE AUTHOR

Jessica Cage is an International Award Winning, and USA Today Best-Selling Author. Born and raised in Chicago, IL, writing has always been a passion for her. She dabbles in artistic creations of all sorts, but it's the pen that her hand itches to hold. Jessica had never considered following her dream to be a writer because she was told far too often "There is no money in writing." So she chose the path most often traveled. During pregnancy, she asked herself an important question. How would she be able to inspire her unborn son to follow his dreams and reach for the stars, if she never had the guts to do it herself? Jessica took a risk and unleash the plethora of characters and their crazy adventurous worlds that had previously existed only in her mind into the realm of readers. She did this with hopes to inspire not only her son but herself. Inviting the world to tag along on her journey to become the writer she has always wanted to be. She hopes to continue writing and bringing her signature Caged Fantasies to readers everywhere.

Printed in the USA
CPSIA information can be obtained
at www.ICGtesting.com
LVHW061318071023
760211LV00001B/140

9 781958 295250